dear reader,

A HARDENED WARRIOR

Clan Ross

Book Two

enjoy!

Hildie McQueen

© Copyright 2020 by Hildie McQueen
Text by Hildie McQueen
Cover by Dar Albert

Dragonblade Publishing, Inc. is an imprint of Kathryn Le Veque Novels, Inc.
P.O. Box 7968
La Verne CA 91750
ceo@dragonbladepublishing.com

Produced in the United States of America

First Edition January 2020
Print Edition

Reproduction of any kind except where it pertains to short quotes in relation to advertising or promotion is strictly prohibited.

All Rights Reserved.

The characters and events portrayed in this book are fictitious. Any similarity to real persons, living or dead, is purely coincidental and not intended by the author.

ARE YOU SIGNED UP FOR DRAGONBLADE'S BLOG?

You'll get the latest news and information on exclusive giveaways, exclusive excerpts, coming releases, sales, free books, cover reveals and more.

Check out our complete list of authors, too!

No spam, no junk. That's a promise!

Sign Up Here

www.dragonbladepublishing.com

Dearest Reader;

Thank you for your support of a small press. At Dragonblade Publishing, we strive to bring you the highest quality Historical Romance from the some of the best authors in the business. Without your support, there is no 'us', so we sincerely hope you adore these stories and find some new favorite authors along the way.

Happy Reading!

CEO, Dragonblade Publishing

Additional Dragonblade books by Author Hildie McQueen

Clan Ross Series

A Heartless Laird

A Hardened Warrior

***** Please visit Dragonblade's website for a full list of books and authors. Sign up for Dragonblade's blog for sneak peeks, interviews, and more: *****

www.dragonbladepublishing.com

CHAPTER ONE

WAS THIS TO be the end of his life? Tristan Ross lay dying on a cot in a cottage somewhere deep in the forest not too far from his home. Where exactly, he would probably never know.

His small party had been ambushed and outnumbered by McLeod warriors. It was a short but brutal attack, which somehow left him injured and alone in the forest. How it happened, he wasn't quite sure.

Interestingly enough, the small party he'd been escorting had been on their way to discuss a truce with the McLeod. With only a few guards, along with his uncle and a woman, they'd not considered that the other clan would consider the group a threat.

Somehow the McLeods had known of their approach and whoever the traitor within his clan was, Tristan wished him the worst. If somehow he managed to survive, which was doubtful, he'd ensure to find the bastard and kill him with his own bare hands.

Darkness beckoned with promises of relief from the pain and Tristan couldn't help but allow the pull. Just as he was about to let out a long breath that would have, in all probability, been his last, a soft jostle brought him back to the present.

Although minute, the movement caused him pain and created the inability to breathe properly. Air wheezed from his lungs and he attempted to groan, but even that was impossible.

The wounds he'd sustained were like none before and because of it, his life ebbed. Tristan sensed the end and grieved at never seeing his family again. He'd never mount his brave warhorse or swim in the icy waters of the nearby loch again.

He was a warrior and to die from wounds was not something to mourn, Tristan reminded himself. At the same time, a warrior did not lie about letting anything or anyone take them without a fight.

"Can ye open yer eyes?" A soft feminine voice permeated through the fog. It was as if stones had been placed on his eyes and no matter how hard he tried, it was impossible to open them.

"Drink this. Ye must try."

Liquid dribbled past his parched lips and down his throat. He drank greedily and wanted to beg for more when it stopped. However, speech evaded him.

Where am I? Tristan tried to ask, but all he managed was a grunt and whoever the woman was, she patted his shoulder.

Cool rags were placed upon his brow, soothing the heat that filled him and lulling him once again to the darkness.

The last thing he wanted was to go to sleep. It could mean death. The only option he would accept was to remain awake, and demand word be sent to his brother, Malcolm, Clan Ross' laird.

Malcolm would come for him. Of that, Tristan was sure. His brother would take him home to die.

"YE HAVE TO wake and tell me how to get news to yer family." The same feminine voice woke him once again. Tristan wasn't aware if it had been days or only hours since the last time he'd heard her.

In the haze of the days since arriving there, he'd caught glimpses of the woman. Or perhaps it had been an illusion. Nothing was certain.

However, he recalled a beautiful, green-eyed Fae hovering over him.

Surely it was not real. The idea of a Fae caring for him was no doubt a hallucination brought on by fever. Perhaps, even now, he imagined it. She'd been hazy, almost as if in a mist, which meant that there was a distinct possibility her appearance was imaginary.

"He is not getting better. We must take him somewhere else to die. If he is found here, we can be accused of killing him," a male voice said.

A soft, cool hand cupped his jaw. "He is not as fevered. However, ye are right. We do need to find his kin. No doubt, they search for him." The woman sounded contrite.

Tristan wondered if the couple was husband and wife.

"I will go see if I can find out something. He will be fine alone. Ye should go home, Merida," the man said in a strong tone. "I will not have ye remain here alone with him."

Merida. The name suited the image he'd either seen or imagined.

The cloth on his brow was replaced. "There, now sleep and get better. Ye must recover to be reunited with yer family. Ye are strong and I am sure ye will live if ye try harder." Her voice so close to his ear was like a balm and Tristan let out a sigh.

She hesitated and seemed to speak to the man. "Ye're right. I best go."

Tristan wanted to beg her to remain, but couldn't muster more than a moan. And then he heard a soft chuckle.

"If ye are trying to say something, ye have to do better." She took his right hand. "Squeeze my hand if ye are from Clan McLeod."

He didn't even try to move his hand.

"Clan Ross?"

The attempt must have worked, because she inhaled sharply. "I see. I am not sure I can find someone to get a message to yer clan. They are not receptive to messengers."

Footsteps neared. "I will take him to them. Tis best he dies there with his kin." The man sounded determined.

The woman let out a breath. "'Tis dangerous. They are known to kill messengers. I cannot allow ye to do it," the woman replied in a soft tone. Tristan loved the sound of it.

"I know someone close to the Ross. If luck is with me, I will find her."

The room became silent. Tristan realized they'd gone outside. Not that it mattered as he couldn't remain awake much longer.

MERIDA MCLEOD'S FEET were like blocks of ice and the weight of them, along with the dampness at the bottom of her skirts, made it hard to continue forward. Every step was a struggle. She trudged toward McLeod Keep on a well-worn path between it and the cottage in the woods where her friend, Grier, a monk, lived.

She'd met the monk while hunting for healing herbs and they'd built a rapport of sorts. He taught her about the healing properties of plants and, in return, she'd brought the older man food, bread or whatever she could sneak from the kitchen.

Her heart pounded. She'd not meant to linger away from home so long and now there was a chance she'd be discovered.

Neither her father nor her brothers would hesitate to lock Merida in her chambers for escaping unescorted. If not holding her captive, they'd assign a guard to follow her every move. Normally, it would be a bother, but not something she'd resent.

However, now that she knew the identity of the injured man, it was good fortune she'd not been caught escaping.

Now, she had to ensure not to be caught coming or going, as she'd either be locked up or guarded.

Neither option was acceptable. She'd promised Grier to return the following day to help move the injured warrior to a cart so he could take the man to the Ross Keep.

If the man lived, which she sincerely doubted, would he remember her? Somehow, she'd known a part of him remained coherent, although he could not speak or breathe properly. What would happen if he did recognize her one day? Hopefully, it would not be in a public forum where he would expose her in front of her father.

Merida worried about Grier. The old man was just stubborn enough to take the injured man to the Ross on his own. Her lips thinned at recalling having found the injured Ross warrior.

It had been during one of their walks that she and Grier spotted the injured man. Together, they'd struggled for what seemed like hours to carry the large, muscled man to Grier's cottage.

Deep in thought, she didn't keep an eye on the path and her foot caught on a limb and she stumbled forward, falling onto the cold ground. "God's foot!" she exclaimed and scrambled to her feet. This was ridiculous. She'd make sure to wear thicker socks with her fur-lined boots the next day.

"Where have ye been?" Ethan, her brother, stood next to a tree.

Merida yelped in fright. Eyes wide and right hand planted over her chest, she glared at him. "Ye scared me half to death," she hissed. "What are ye doing out here?"

"Merida." Ethan's narrowed eyes traveled over her before landing on her empty basket.

"Who are ye feeding?"

"An old man. He teaches me about herbs in return." She told the truth since whenever she tried to lie her face would turn red and blotchy.

Ethan neared and took her arm. "Father will forget ye are a woman and beat yer bum raw if he finds out." Her brother pulled her roughly to a side gate that was hidden by overgrown bushes. "Ye best hope he doesn't see ye."

When she attempted to pull her arm away, he held fast. "I won't tell anyone this time. But let it be yer last time out. Tis too dangerous."

"I cannot let someone starve to death. Tis impossible to find food when the weather turns so cold."

Ethan lifted a brow. Her brother was ruthless and cruel. Rarely was he kind to anyone. On more than one occasion, she'd intervened when he'd beaten servants mercilessly for minor transgressions while doing simple chores.

It surprised her when he nodded. "I suppose. However, next time take a guard with ye. Tis too dangerous," he repeated and looked past her, seeming to lose interest in the conversation. No doubt, something weighed on his mind, otherwise, he would not have hesitated to announce what she did to their father.

Their ongoing war with Clan Ross was always foremost in everyone's thoughts. Ethan didn't have to clarify why it was dangerous for anyone to leave the safety of the keep. Merida bit her lip to keep from blurting the conflict was his fault.

Instead, she hitched her chin. "I find it quite odd that ye be out here yerself."

His expression shuttered. "Tis none of yer concern."

"Tell me, Brother. Who are ye meeting?"

"Merida," he growled. "Keep this up and I will inform father of yer outings."

She couldn't risk it. "Fine." Slipping through the gate, she hurried to the side garden and to a small shed where she placed her basket on a shelf.

The entrance to the kitchen beckoned. It was risky to be caught entering from outdoors if her mother was there, but her stomach growled. The door creaked, opening to a huge, activity-filled kitchen. Rose, the cook, stirred something in a pot, while a servant girl chopped noisily. Another sat in the corner churning butter, her face bright with perspiration.

"Child, come and stand by the hearth. Whatever were ye doing out in the frigid weather?" Rose chided while continuing to stir. Her normally bright red cheeks gave her a friendly appearance.

The cook then motioned to a young woman who walked in with an armful of chopped wood. "Put that by the hearth and serve Mistress Merida some hot porridge."

Rose moved away from the pot, wiping her hands on the front of a long apron. "I will pour ye a bit of honeyed mead to warm yer bones."

After pulling a chair closer to the fire, Merida slipped her feet from the sodden socks and shoes and held them up to the warmth. She sighed happily as the heat seeped into her. "I love ye, Rose," she said, reaching for the cup the cook offered.

Rose neared and whispered into her ear, "Ye need to stop skulking about in the woods. One day, ye will find trouble."

Pretending not to hear, Merida drank the mead, leaning forward so the heat of the fire could help warm her hands and face.

"There will only be ten of us for the midday meal." Merida's mother's voice was like a closed fist to the stomach, but Merida refused to turn around. Her mother could always tell if she was hiding something. And the last thing Merida wanted was to worry her.

Instead, Merida tucked her feet under the chair, hoping to hide the dirty hem of her skirts. She watched the servant churn, the paddle moving up and down. Up and down.

"Merida?" Her mother neared. "Whatever are ye doing lingering about?"

"I am hungry so I came for a bit of porridge." Again, it was the truth.

Her mother tapped Merida's shoulder. "Nonsense. Ye can wait until the midday meal. Come along, dear."

"I missed my morning meal."

"Tis what happens when ye linger in bed until all hours and then spend half the day out in the corrals with that devil of a horse. Ye are not a lad, Merida."

Her mother believed her when she claimed she wanted to spend time practicing archery or riding her horse, Duin, around the corral.

Duin was a stubborn beast that refused to allow anyone but her to care for him. So most mornings, she had to spend time with the unruly beast. It was a chore at times, but Merida enjoyed having something to do that allowed her out of the confines of the dreary, cold keep.

She plodded after her mother, barefoot. "Where are we going?"

"Yer father wishes to speak to ye."

Her heart threatened to stop and she gasped for breath. "About what?" She stopped at the end of the corridor that led to her father's study.

"Ye know." Her mother's expression softened and there was a slight curve at the edges of her lips. Merida had inherited her mother's fair skin and bright red hair. However, her mother's blue eyes were a slightly different shade of blue than Merida's.

Merida refused to take a step further. "I will not marry a Mackenzie."

"This is not a discussion to have with me, Child. Ye know yer father will have the final say in whom ye marry. Tis time, Merida; we have given you more than enough leave. Come, yer father waits."

She'd also inherited her mother's stubborn nature, which made for interesting exchanges between them. "Ye promised to speak to him."

"Merida!" Her father's voice boomed right behind her and Merida jumped.

"Why is everyone trying to scare me to death today?" Merida exclaimed. "I will not have it." She attempted to skirt around her father, but he was quick and took her by the arm and guided her into his study.

"Tis time to settle ye," he said without preamble. "And it is also time for this war between our clans to stop. I will send a messenger to the Mackenzie and ask for ye and yer mother to visit for the season. Prepare yer things. Ensure to take gowns suitable for…" He waved his hand in the air and looked to his wife for help. Both Merida and her mother looked at him, unsure what he meant to say.

"Oh, ye know, clothing for men to notice ye," his father finished gruffly and cleared his throat.

Despite the situation, Merida smiled at his discomfort. "So ye wish men to notice me now, do ye, Da?"

Her father glared at her. "Only whoever ye will marry."

"Come along," her mother said. "We have much to do and the day is half over." Her keen eyes narrowed at Merida's bare feet. "Why are ye barefoot?"

Pretending not to hear, Merida looked to her father. "I wish to marry a man of my choosing."

"Ye have a duty to the clan," her father replied, his gaze steadfast.

All her life, she'd been groomed to be the wife of either a laird or high-standing man. Although she'd always wished for a choice of husband, Merida had always known this day would come. She pictured the eligible Mackenzies and had to admit most were attractive men. Only two of the laird's sons remained single. However, she didn't think the Mackenzie would marry her to either. No, she'd be married to a nephew or, perhaps, a bastard-born son.

Letting out a sigh, she trudged through the great room and down a corridor into her chamber and looked around the orderly space.

First, she'd remove the soiled gown and after changing, she'd send a messenger to Grier. She pictured the dying warrior back in the cabin. He was handsome, strong and his body was very enticing. It had been impossible not to notice as she'd cleaned his wounds and helped Grier with stitching them closed. They'd turned him onto his side to wash him and she'd bitten her lip at the sight of his plump, round bottom.

Whoever he was would definitely be someone she could see as a bed partner.

"Merida?" Her mother's voice made her jump. When she rounded Merida and looked at her, it was almost comical. "Have ye gone daft, Child? Why are ye standing there with yer dress half off, staring at the wall?"

It was one of her favorite things, to make her mother blush. "I was thinking of a man's naked bottom."

As always, her mother's cheeks turned a bright red. "Honestly, Merida, the things ye say." Her mother took her by the shoulders and gave her a gentle push. "I will fetch Elsa and Paige to come keep ye company while ye pack," her mother said, referring to her companion and eldest brother's new wife.

THE NEXT MORNING brought heavy snow and a frigid wind that halted all the plans for travel. Merida looked out the window at the falling flakes and wondered what Grier would do.

She'd received a reprieve until spring. However, once spring came, there would be no excuse for not marrying.

Ross Keep

EVERY SECOND OF the day became unbearable. Each breath and attempt to move was excruciating for Tristan. Days or perhaps weeks had passed, he had no way of knowing.

The only thing he did know now was the constant wish for death. Anything was better than living like he was. Unable to move, talk or see. Whenever he was moved or jostled, he screamed silently, knowing outwardly all they saw were the salty tears that fell past his parched lips.

"Tristan, open yer eyes."

"Tristan, can ye hear me?"

Why did they not help him die? End the torture of his existence? He tried to tell them, fought to open his eyes but, as always, nothing happened.

For some reason, he'd lost control of his body. Nothing obeyed his commands to move, open or speak. Weak from lack of nourishment and lying upon a bed for so long, he could not take anything more.

He shivered when wet cloths wiped down his face and body and groaned when they turned him to clean his back.

"Tristan, are ye cold?"

"Drink this. Slowly."

His mother's voice permeated the air and he almost smiled. He pried his eyes open and was just able to see her face. She didn't seem different, not aged nor raged with concern. No, she seemed more curious than anything as she smiled at him. "There ye are, Lad. Drink this broth now."

Perhaps he drank, or maybe not. All the he knew for certain was that the pain didn't ebb.

SOMETHING JOSTLED HIM out of slumber and Tristan frowned. He opened his eyes to find a dark hound turning in circles on the bed, trying to find a comfortable spot. The beast paid him little heed, too intent on ensuring the perfect spot to lie.

"Titus." Tristan's voice was gruff with lack of use. "What are ye doing?"

The dog cocked its head and studied him, then got to its feet and leaned over him, the dark eyes meeting his. It gave a low whine and, to Tristan's surprise, the hound licked his face once and then returned to the quest for a perfect place to sleep.

When it finally settled right next to his side, it let out a sigh and placed its large head on Tristan's thigh.

The animal's warmth seeped into his body, giving him comfort. In that moment, Tristan realized the pain had ebbed enough that it wasn't the first thing on his mind. Lips curving, he allowed slumber to overtake him.

Chapter Two

Spring

WITH THE GRACE of a highborn, Paige made her way through the people in the great room, her gaze on him the entire time. Alec McLeod was proud of his choice for wife. More than that, he was eager for nights when she slept tucked against him for warmth.

Their marriage had been hurried and without much fanfare as they'd been in the middle of a clan war. Unlike most women that married a first-born son to a laird, Paige had not resented the lack of festivities. Instead, she was more relieved than anything at not being the center of attention.

His lips curved. When she passed by, men did their best not to gawk at the beauty, but few were successful. Even in the muted dress she wore that evening, she was lovely. Her gaze lifted up to meet his, the pools of blue seeming to sparkle in the candlelight as she neared.

"How fare ye, Husband?" Her soft murmur ran though Alec's body as if she'd touched him.

Unable to stop from it, he leaned close and pressed his lips to just below her ear. "Much better now that I see ye."

A light blush surfaced on her cheeks and her eyes rounded. "Alec, people are watching."

"Let them," he said and pulled her chair back to allow her to sit.

Last meal could not end quick enough in his opinion. He'd been absent for several days, riding with some of his guards, ensuring their borders were secure now that spring deemed to make its appearance.

A guard approached the high board and waited for Laird McLeod to acknowledge him.

Alec's father washed down his last bite with ale and motioned the guard closer. "What is it, Jonathan?"

"A messenger has arrived, Laird."

"Send him to my study." Alec's father looked to him. "Let us go see about this. It may be important since the messenger was sent as soon as traveling became possible."

Before standing, Alec turned to Paige and once again pressed his lips to the side of her neck.

"Go," Paige whispered, gently pushing him back.

Alec couldn't help but chuckle at how shy she was. He loved that about her. Especially since, although timid, she was also curious about bed sport and passionate when making love.

Along with his father, he walked into the study to find a large, muscular man escorted by two of their guards. Unlike most messengers, who were normally younger guardsmen, this one seemed seasoned with an unwavering gaze.

There was a slight tic at his jaw, telling them that he was not used to the task of messenger. Alec studied the man with curiosity. By the colors of the tartan that crossed his broad chest, he was definitely not a Ross.

"I come with a message from the Mackenzie," the man said without preamble, not waiting for the laird to allow him to speak.

Alec had to admire the man's lack of decorum. He was often accused of such himself. It seemed his father didn't mind it either as he went to the sideboard and poured a glass of whisky and handed it to the messenger. "To warm ye up."

"Thank ye," the large man said and swallowed the liquid down in two gulps.

"What is the message?" Alec asked.

The guard then assumed a rigid pose, his intent gaze meeting first Alec's and then his father's. "He requests yer presence within three days, if possible."

Once the message was delivered, the messenger was invited to remain and eat. The man requested to eat in the kitchens and be allowed to take food for two other men who waited outside.

Alec walked with him.

"I will send for yer men. Why did ye come? Tis obvious ye are a warrior."

"My laird wasn't sure how unstable yer region was." The man met his gaze. "Ye are in the midst of war. He wanted to ensure the message was received."

They entered the kitchen and Alec motioned a young lad forward. "Retrieve the other two men to come inside to eat."

"Thank ye," the messenger nodded to Alec. "I am Gaeden."

"Alec," the laird's son responded.

"Ye may remain the night," Alec invited as per Highland tradition.

"We shall and leave first thing in the morning."

Once the men were settled around a small table, Alec spoke to Rose and requested that food be prepared for their travel the next day.

He headed to his father's study and found the McLeod remained standing next to the side table, his expression thoughtful.

"Why do ye think the Mackenzie sends for us to come?" Alec poured whisky into a small cup. "Tis not a social call it seems."

His father shook his head. "No, it must have something to do with the battle between us and Clan Ross. If I know the Mackenzie, he will try to gain something from it. Perhaps our alliance or acquiescence to fall under his command."

"Never," Alec responded, looking to the whisky and assessing whether to have another glass. Deciding against it, he put his cup down. "Father, we must contact the McLeods from the east. They are large and can help."

When his father blew out a breath and nodded, Alec could almost feel the weight upon his shoulders. "They will not help. Not after what Ethan did. He left yer cousin a cripple by cheating at the games."

"He brings us so much trouble. And yet, there is little we can do about it now."

They would never turn Ethan over to either the other Laird McLeod or to the Ross. He was the second son born to a laird and, although Alec knew his father had contemplated it, it would not happen.

Regardless of his many faults, Ethan was his son.

"We set for the Mackenzie lands tomorrow. Ensure guardsmen are prepared. I will speak to yer mother as she wishes to go as well."

ALTHOUGH THERE WAS a fire in the hearth, the chamber was chilly and Paige hurried to wash up before going to bed. Knowing Alec would be joining her that night, she took extra care to ensure her body was clean. By the time she completed the task and pulled on her chemise, she was shivering and went closer to the fire in the hearth.

Alec entered, his gaze intent on her. Standing before the fireplace, she realized he was privy to an outline of her body through the folds of her chemise.

It was hard not to rush to him and remove his clothing, her need growing as he pinned her with a darkened gaze.

"Beautiful," he said, his gaze roaming down her body. "Loosen yer hair."

Although she'd just braided her hair, she didn't resent the request, quite the opposite. Tingles of awareness traveled through her as she ran her fingers through the tresses, allowing them to catch the light.

Playfully, she pulled it up and then allowed it to cascade down past her shoulders to the center of her back. "I missed ye, Husband."

Not nearing, Alec yanked his tunic up over his head, his breeches following quickly thereafter. Wonderfully nude, he was on full display for her perusal.

"See how I want ye," he said unnecessarily as Paige couldn't help but notice his member was hard, straight and erect. That she had this effect on the powerful male never ceased to amaze her.

Paige approached and looked up at him. "I want ye as much."

Alec's mouth crashed over hers, his tongue immediately seeking purchase past her lips and she allowed it, sucking greedily, needing to taste him.

"Mmm," she purred and ran her hands down his back to the roundness of his buttocks. Once there, she dug her fingernails into the skin, needing to pull him closer against her. Paige rose to her tiptoes in an effort to align her sex with his. Unfortunately, he was too tall.

It was only when her chemise pooled at her feet that Paige realized he'd disrobed her. She barely paid any heed, much too consumed with the feel of his skin against every inch of hers.

The roughness of his palms as he ran them down her sides sent quivers of anticipation through her body and Paige arched against him.

The assault of his mouth continued, traveling from her now swollen lips, past her jawline to the base of Paige's throat.

All the while, she raked her hands down his back, needing more than what he gave at the moment and yet hoping it would not stop. The longer this moment was prolonged, the more she'd enjoy what was to come. And yet, her urgent need was more than Paige could stand.

Alec dipped at the knees and hoisted her up and Paige wrapped her legs around his midsection. Both were impatient, dripping with need and unable to stop from immediately joining. Lowering her to the bed, he positioned himself and drove into her so deep that she gasped at the delightful intrusion.

Both groaned in relief and, immediately, Alec began pumping in and out with the frantic rhythm of lovers separated for far too long.

"Oh, yes!" Paige exclaimed, urging his movements, her crest coming so quickly it took her breath away. He slid his hands under her bottom, lifting her for better access. When he drew out and thrust back in, she dissolved into the abyss of stars and darkness, her body flying with a climax so hard, she thought never to return from it.

As Paige floated down, Alec continued his own quest, turning her onto her stomach. Then he lifted her up into position to make it easier to enter her from behind.

Paige cried out, overwhelmed with arousal once again. The edges of the bedding bunched under her palms as she grappled to remain in place while her husband pumped in and out of her, his thrusts hard and steady.

His fingers digging into Paige's hips, Alec held her firmly in place as he desperately sought release, seeming to find it elusive. His member was hard and thick, filling her completely and sending her to, once again, lose all control.

Finally, as she cried out in a second overwhelming release, he plunged one last time, his hold firm on her body as his hoarse cry echoed in the room.

Trembling, he collapsed sideways, bringing her with him. They lay spooned, him behind her, his sex firmly inside her body, claiming her, unrelenting.

Lazily, he stroked her breasts, his thumb circling her tip, first one and then the other, sending a new tingle of awareness down from where he touched her to her stomach and then on past.

It amazed her how Alec could bring her to want, over and over again, using different tactics to drive her to madness.

When he slid his hand down her stomach to in between her legs, she pushed back, taking more of him in. Already, his member was hardening. And while Paige's need renewed, at the same time she wasn't sure she could take much more.

Gently, he parted her nether lips and found her more sensitive part. His finger slid up and down over it and Paige gasped as new ripples of excitement filled her.

"Oh!" she gasped when his finger moved over the now tight bud over and over.

Knowing what she would need, Alec pulled out just a bit and pushed back into her, the move slower this time, the rhythm steady.

They continued in the lazy lovemaking until needing to find release minutes later.

"Ye drive me to madness," Alec whispered in her ear, guiding her to lie back onto the bedding.

Her mouth fell open as Alec came over her. Once he lifted her legs over his shoulders, he drove into her wetness.

For a third time, Paige became lost in the wilderness of lust and passion.

CHAPTER THREE

HAD HIS SWORD always been so heavy? Tristan swung, his entire arm quivering as contact was made with the opponent's weapon.

"Ye are recovering well," Ruari, his cousin, yelled over the sound of other warriors practicing. "But ye need to gain weight."

Tristan looked down at his sunken stomach and gaunt chest. In the last month, he'd eaten as much as possible to regain his strength, but it was taking time after so many weeks of eating little more than broth. Not one to complain, he shrugged and teased. "Once I do, ye will run from me."

In truth, Ruari was the only one he preferred to spar with. Because of Tristan's large size, the other guardsmen usually did not present much of a challenge. Kieran was as strong and almost his height, but they'd ended up brawling on the ground so many times that their father had forbidden they spar against one another.

Just a few yards from him, Kieran sparred against two guardsmen. In his element, he made loud noises when on the attack and was deft to avoid the strikes when the men countered.

Although head of the archers, Kieran held his own with the sword. Seeming to sense his regard, his brother looked toward him and then uncharacteristically scanned him over as if ensuring he was well.

Despite the lack of strength, his family made Tristan strong within. His body would continue to recover and, eventually, like before, he would wield the sword without thought of its weight.

Moira, the cook, sent a maid to announce last meal and the men made their way to the dining hall, each man either placing his sword in a scabbard across his back or holding it to the side.

They lined up just outside the front entry. Two barrels were filled with water from the loch. A stack of neatly folded cloths had been placed on a weathered table next to the barrels that were dipped to wash away sweat and dirt or used for drying.

Some bypassed the barrels. Others, like Tristan, waited patiently for those who'd arrived first to finish so they could use the water. Unused to the exertion of sword practice, sweat dripped from him like water, making the wait to wash up a necessity. As hungry as he was, the idea of sweat dripping into his food was unappetizing.

"Where is Malcolm?" Kieran came up from behind. Unlike him, the younger man didn't seem as spent. Although his broad chest did lift and lower continuously from the exercise, his brother looked renewed and unhindered by the fact he carried not just his sword, but his bow and quiver as well.

"Inside, I suppose," Tristan replied. "Why?"

Kieran didn't reply at first. Instead, his steady hazel gaze moved to the doorway. Finally, after the barrel was available for them to use, his brother spoke. "He is sending me to the north post. Probably to keep me away as spring comes."

It was a true statement, but Tristan wasn't about to say anything to his short-tempered brother.

The low growl of Kieran's complaint made it evident his brother was not pleased at the assignment.

Tristan understood why Malcolm felt the need to send the youngest away. It would help keep the clan war at bay a bit longer.

Tension between Clans Ross and McLeod meant the weak truce between them, mostly due to winter, could easily be broken. Although there was no doubt in Tristan's mind they would battle again, both clans needed time to recover after a long season of war.

He studied Kieran for a moment.

"Ye are needed at the northern post. Warm weather always brings with it threats of the Norse attacks. If Malcolm allows it, I will go in yer stead."

"Ye know damned well he won't allow it. Tis my need for revenge that he fears. That I will do something to cause the war to start anew."

The water in the trough was frigid and just what was needed. The brothers washed up in silence.

After, they made their way through the wide archway into the keep. Its thick, wooden door was left open to allow for fresh air into the dim, smoky interior.

Flames from candles in wall sconces flickered in the breeze as they walked past. The sounds of plates and cups against wooden tables filled the room in an almost musical rhythm.

Holding trays of trenchers of food high, servants weaved through the room, making their way down the rows of tables, deftly stepping over dogs, babes and spills.

People ate while conversing, interrupting the dialog with long draws from tankards and cups. In the center of the room, a child that cried loudly suddenly stopped when the mother lifted it up to her lap.

Tristan's first inclination was to sit with the other guardsmen. But upon inspection, the table was already filled. An archer circled another table and sat down, not leaving room for him there either.

"Ye can sit here," a comely woman invited, motioning to a small, but empty space next to her. Tristan peered down her blouse when she leaned forward, exposing her ample bosom.

"Thank ye." He sat at the edge of the bench when she slid over. The space was so tight that she was plastered against him, which neither of them minded.

"Yer brother request ye come up to the high board," a young maid said as she tapped Tristan on the shoulder.

The woman next to him whimpered. "I was hoping to speak with ye," she murmured.

"I will come and find ye later," Tristan replied, knowing exactly what they planned to do. It had little to do with speaking. The woman's lips curved in response.

He walked up to the high board noting Kieran was already being served. The loud rumblings from his stomach made him glad food was already waiting at his place.

"Is there a reason both of ye avoid sitting here?" The deep timbre in Malcolm's voice was a sure sign his brother was not in a good mood. "Ye are the laird's brothers."

Tristan and Kieran exchanged glances, each hoping the other would reply to their brother. When Kieran remained silent, Tristan replied.

"I was simply hoping to find company for the night." He did his best not to grin, knowing it would only make Malcolm angrier.

"I came up here directly," Kieran said.

"Only after ye couldn't squeeze in at the archers' table."

Both looked to the table where the archers made a comical sight. They sat so close together that their elbows touched whenever they brought food to their mouths.

"Why are so many people here today?" Tristan asked, annoyed that he couldn't eat in peace. The lamb stew was delicious, served with freshly-baked bread slathered with creamy, churned butter. He dipped bread into the broth and bit into it.

"I held hearings all day and my wife invited almost every family with concerns to remain for the meal. She said people looked gaunt," Malcolm grumbled. "They look fine to me."

This time, all three studied the families who ate with gusto, most barely lifting their heads except to mumble a word or two.

With their mother and sister gone to visit cousins, the control of the kitchens and household was placed on the shoulders of Malcolm's wife, Elspeth. The beauty was a gifted healer but, in Tristan's opinion, too softhearted to be a laird's wife.

Since she'd arrived, the hound population had tripled. And they'd taken in lame horses, which enjoyed daily feedings and the expanse of the clan's corrals.

In addition, two cottages had been built for foundlings and orphaned children, who were being watched over by newly-hired women to oversee their care.

Sitting on the end of the table chatting happily with her best friend, Ceilidh, Elspeth seemed oblivious to the chaos of the room. Instead, they smiled, watching a babe toddle down an aisle until landing on its bottom and bringing bread to its mouth.

Just then, a guard approached.

"Laird, a messenger from the Mackenzie is here."

Immediately, all three brothers tensed.

Malcolm motioned the messenger, who remained at the doorway, forward.

The young man looked around the room with a confused expression. Being they had a reputation for being ruthless and hardened, the somewhat festive atmosphere didn't suit.

"What say ye?" Malcolm asked the messenger in a low voice, signaling that the messenger should speak softly and not be overheard by those nearby.

The young man pulled a missive from a sack that hung from a strap across his body and held it out to Malcolm. "Greetings from my laird, the Mackenzie."

"Stay and eat. If ye can find a space," Malcolm said, scanning the room. "Perhaps ye would prefer the kitchen," he added and motioned a maid over.

The young man's face brightened. No doubt, he was ravenous after a long day's ride. Surprisingly, he was quickly seated with a family who made room for him.

Malcolm tore the wax seal and read the message. He then folded it and tucked it into his belt. "After the meal, come to my study," he said and then leaned forward and repeated the same to their uncle.

Letting out a breath that he could finish his meal, Tristan returned his attention to the food on his plate.

After the meal, Tristan meandered toward the study. He slowed next to the table where the woman who'd offered him a seat remained.

He leaned forward to whisper in her ear. "What is yer name?"

"Adele," she replied with a saucy smile.

"Please remain here for the night. I am sure we can assure ye accommodations," he continued, not particularly caring that Malcolm glared in his direction.

The atmosphere in the study was tense, curiosity the only thing keeping everyone quiet. Along with Kieran and his uncle, Gregor, Ruari was also present. It was rare that his cousin would be in attendance, the loner usually rebuffing any invitation to attend to family gatherings and such.

Malcolm pulled the missive from his belt. "The Mackenzie requests our presence. According to this," he lifted the parchment, "he wishes to discuss the ongoing clan war between us and the McLeods."

"What business is it of his?" Kieran bit out. "He has made some sort of pact with the McLeod, I have no doubt."

Gregor Ross, the late laird's brother, shook his head. "Not necessarily. Yer father and the Mackenzie were good friends. If anything, he is requesting peace since both of our clans are in alliance with them."

"To what means?" Tristan asked. "We have little to do with them and he does not need us."

Malcolm cleared his throat. "The Mackenzie will use the dispute between our clans to his advantage. He will offer payments and purchases of land under the guise of wishing peace when what he really wants is to grow his territory."

"Our fight is not about land. Tis about revenge, ensuring those dogs pay for killing Da," Kieran said, his face twisted in anger. "Send back the message that we are not interested in hearing what he has to offer."

Malcolm shook his head. "Tis not so simple." He turned to Tristan. "What say ye about this?

"That we should make a show of accepting his invitation, listen to what he has to say. A McLeod will likely be there as well, so this will give us the opportunity to learn what they plan."

"My thoughts exactly," Gregor said. "I believe McLeod asked the Mackenzie for reinforcements, but instead they offer talks."

Kieran stalked toward the door.

"When do ye leave for the north post?" Malcolm asked.

The youngest barely slowed his pace. "Two days hence."

For a moment, no one spoke. Finally, Gregor looked to Malcolm. "I advise against ye going. Send either me or Tristan."

"I will go," Tristan offered. He was ready to learn what he could and ensure they were informed of what the McLeod planned. "If the McLeod went to the Mackenzie to ask for help, it begs to ask, who else are they seeking assistance from?"

Although Clan Ross was formidable in size, boasting over five hundred warriors, Clan Mackenzie's force was double the size.

Preferring to remain at peace with the powerful clan, they'd entered an alliance a decade earlier. Since then, there'd never been any problems between them.

The Mackenzie and their father had become friends over the years. However, only a fool would put his full faith in the powerful man. Known for being ruthless and preferring power over anything else, the Mackenzie's reputation was not one of a being fair.

"Ye can go. Take Ruari and Ian, along with twenty guards."

Tristan nodded and looked to his cousin, who seemed more shocked than pleased. "Can ye survive without yer horses for longer than a sennight?" he teased the sullen man.

"Tis not the horses I miss, tis being around other people that I can't abide," the large man snarled. "Mackenzies especially."

CHAPTER FOUR

DUIN, MERIDA'S HORSE, moved with the fluidity that told of its fulfilled desire to be outdoors and without the boundaries of a corral or stable stall. Merida gave it leave to keep its own pace, knowing that although the beast would push boundaries, it would be forever mindful and not do anything to hurt her.

Whether her parents and guards grew more annoyed with the distance she kept ahead of the party did not bother her in the least. It was, perhaps, to be one of the last times she'd have the freedom to be alone, riding without the restraints of a husband, no obligations to anyone or anything.

Her hair came loose from its bindings as the wind ripped through it and she laughed at the idea of her appearance upon arriving at Mackenzie Keep. Hair loosed, gown askew, breathless and upon a sweaty animal, surely the last thing on anyone's mind would be that she, the daughter of a less than influential laird, would make a good match for a Mackenzie.

Duin slowed and she sensed the approach of a rider. Her brother, Ethan, came alongside. Why he'd come was anyone's guess. Probably her father's attempt to keep him from doing more harm. The fragile truce between her clan and the Ross' would not last now that spring arrived. It would take little to fan the embers into another raging fire of battles, death and suffering.

As it was, their clan was barely able to survive, the effects of Ethan's rash action rippling through each and every clansperson. Even now, their courtyard was overfilled by those displaced by the clan war. Women attempting to find a way in life without a husband, having to feed their children, clung to what they could to make life normal again. Meanwhile, confused orphaned children scraped by on a daily existence of what they could scavenge.

It was a sad affair, a daily reminder of the harshness of life. Merida slid a glance to Ethan, who sat straight upon his steed. With burnished brown waves down to his wide shoulders, he made for a handsome sight. His gaze was always flat, unyielding, and his expression was usually stoic.

All her life, Merida had known her brother was not a good person, sometimes even fearing him for the cruelty he would display against not just animals, but other people. And yet she kept a place in her heart open to him in hopes that, one day, he'd allow kindness to seep in and touch what was deeply buried within.

"Ye have to slow. We will rest just over the ridge there," Ethan said, pointing to a slope not too far away. "If ye break yer neck, Mother will be most displeased."

"Would ye be as well?" She looked to him, waiting for a response. Perhaps he'd surprise her again like he'd done when finding out she'd stolen away from the keep while caring for the injured warrior.

He shrugged. "Not particularly. It would be yer fault." With that, he rode ahead, holding up a hand to signal to the guards where they'd stop. She followed his progress as he circled to a shallow creek and dismounted. Jaw set, his upper lip curled in distaste when two guards laughed about something. In that moment, Merida felt sorry for her brother. How could a person not find at least a bit of joy in life? Her brother's view on life made her sad.

When she dismounted and guided Duin to the water's edge, her mother hurriedly neared. With an expression akin to someone who'd tasted a bitter fruit, her mother clicked her tongue. "Merida, ye look a fright. It will not do for ye to arrive at the keep looking as such. Rinse yer face and wash yer hands and arms. Ye will ride the rest of the day in the wagon with me."

"I prefer to ride..."

"No, we have given ye most of the day upon that dastardly beast. I kept expecting it to throw ye. The animal is more fit for battle than to be ridden by a lass."

Used to her mother's distaste for her affinity for her horse, Merida smiled. "Duin loves me and would never hurt me. Tis the last bit of freedom I may have."

At the softening of her mother's face, Merida felt relief. It was quickly gone, however. "I know, Child. However, ye must be presentable. Remember, not only do we come as guests of the Mackenzie, but also as the wife and daughter of Laird McLeod."

Acknowledging the truth of her mother's words, she let out a sigh. "I will ride with ye." Merida trudged to the water's edge to where her horse had meandered.

Wandering away from the others and taking advantage of the privacy, she relieved herself behind some bushes and then washed up in the clear water. Although frigid, the water felt refreshing and clean. Merida straightened, taking a deep breath.

The chilly breeze blew up from the water to caress her damp face and Merida took a long breath. The combination of blue sky, green trees and water was beautiful. Perhaps she could find Ethan and point her observations out to him.

Her brother didn't acknowledge her approach. He was crouched down, drinking from the creek.

"Did ye notice what a beautiful spot this is?" Merida lowered to her knees and peered at him. "Is it our land?"

Ethan slid a narrowed look in her direction. Not looking around as she'd expected, instead he shrugged. "I believe we are on Mackenzie lands."

"I wish we had a place like this one? Do we?"

Giving her a droll look, he straightened and stretched.

"Merida," her mother called. "Come now."

Taking Duin's reins, she tugged the reluctant animal away from the grasses and back toward where the others were. "Coming, Mother."

MACKENZIE KEEP STOOD proud, perched high on a mountainside, visible from a long distance away. Wide roadways led up to an intimidating set of wooden gates atop which archers remained at the ready.

Outside, on both sides of the gates, were mounted guards keeping watch for any threat. The idea of it was ludicrous. No one in their right mind would ever consider an attack on one of the largest, most powerful clans in the Highlands.

Nonetheless, the impressive show of force and sheer magnitude of archers atop the thick walls surrounding the keep never ceased to fascinate Merida, who'd visited often as a child.

On this day, however, the size of the keep and number of guards had a different effect. It signified more of a prison than a home, a fortress as impossible to get into as it would be to escape from. Heart thundering in her chest, Merida gasped for breath and leaned out the side of the wagon, looking for Duin.

He'd been tethered to one of the guard's horses. It was the third guard to attempt to keep the unruly beast in line. Duin did not take kindly to being tethered to another horse, nor did he particularly care for most men.

"I should see about him," Merida said when her horse bucked and snorted making the equally huge warhorse it was tethered to sidestep.

As if God took pity on Merida, her father had come alongside the wagon atop his own black steed. "See about yer beast. I do not know how ye can make it mind," he grumbled.

Thankful for the opportunity to get away from the confines of the wagon, she jumped down and raced to Duin, barely missing a step and mounting.

"Remain alongside me," her father called, and she rode closer.

The gates to the keep were open and, still, it was as if an invisible wall remained in place. Even after being motioned to enter by guards, Merida held Duin's reins tight, communicating to the horse that it should behave.

Duin, however, cared little for the unfamiliarity of the surroundings and skirted sideways, pawing at the ground to show its displeasure.

"Ye should have left that damned beast behind," Ethan remarked with a frown. "Who is going to care for it here?"

"I will." Merida hitched her chin. She'd purposely brought the horse as an excuse to escape endless hours sitting about stitching, reading or whatever mundane tasks women were often expected to fill their days with.

Duin had always been the balm to long days indoors, which never gave her a true sense of accomplishment. Men had wars, battles, crafts and other activities that gave them purpose. In Merida's opinion, women were expected to do nothing of great value for the clan.

The sun was setting as they dismounted. Her mother, Paige and Elsa, her companion, were assisted from the wagon. Trunks were carried away by lads and maids guided the visitors to the front doorway.

Meanwhile, Merida remained with Duin. She followed behind stable lads and guards, who didn't trust their steeds to other's care and tugged her horse toward the stables.

Once she managed to coax Duin into a stall, she removed the saddle, brushed him down and filled a bucket with fresh oats, another with water. Making eye contact with the horse, she ran a hand down the center of his head and pressed her cheek to his. "Thank you for coming with me," she whispered. "Be a dear and do not fret. I will fetch ye first thing and take ye out."

She dug into a satchel that hung at her waist and pulled out a carrot. "Here ye go."

The animal sniffed it and deemed it worthy, taking delicate bites that never ceased to amuse Merida. For such a huge war beast, he was quite mild when it came to eating.

Merida lingered as the guards left, one by one, until finally leaving her alone. Although she knew her mother would be cross if she didn't get back to the keep soon, Merida lingered, pulling a blanket from the stall and throwing it over Duin's back. It was warm enough that he didn't need it, but the night would bring a chill and the animal had traveled a long distance. Besides, she liked to pamper it.

"Have a good night's rest, Duin," she told the horse who gave her a bored look.

"Does yer horse ever reply?"

Merida whipped around and lost her breath. It was Caylen Mackenzie, one of the laird's sons. Of all the worst luck, this one was quite a rogue.

He gave her a bemused look and then allowed his gaze to roam down her body. "Are ye McLeod's lass?"

"Aye, his daughter, Merida," she replied, lifting her chin. "Ye are Caylen, the Mackenzie's second son."

He nodded and studied Duin. "Tis a large horse for a wee lass." He reached to touch Duin, but upon the animal's obvious displeasure, he pulled back. "A rowdy one at that."

She'd attended Caylen's wedding ceremony two years earlier.

He'd been married to a Robertson. A young, plain girl, who'd sniffed through the entire ceremony. At the time, she'd felt bad for both as they went through the ritual of an arranged marriage that would benefit their clans in one way or another.

"How is yer wife, Brenna?"

Caylen let out a noise, almost like the one Duin made when displeased. "She remains at her parents' keep for the most part."

"Do ye regret marrying?" Merida caught herself. "I apologize, tis just that my father seeks to find me a husband and I wish to know what it's like to..."

He met her gaze with flat, blue eyes. "To marry someone ye barely know?" He shrugged. "Tis what ye would expect. Ye get to know one another, see if ye suit. If ye do, then it's good. If ye do not, then one can seek pleasure elsewhere." With each word, he moved closer until Merida was pressed against the stall door.

"I... see," she replied pushing him back. "I best see about greeting yer da with my parents."

Someone cleared their throat and Caylen turned away slowly. Merida tried to look around him as he lifted a hand in greeting, but he was much too tall and broad in the shoulders.

Unable to see whom it was that had entered, Merida decided it was best to take the opportunity and leave. She slipped sideways and out the stables. Skirts lifted, she raced to the keep to ensure her parents would not be too cross by her absence.

"There ye are. I was about to send a guard to hunt for ye." Her mother regarded her from head to toe. "Honestly, Merida, how did yer hair become such a mess in a short time?"

The red waves rarely remained tamed unless they were braided painfully tight. Using both hands, she attempted to smooth the front of her hair down. "There, let us go find Father."

Arm in arm, Merida and her mother crossed the threshold into the great hall behind Laird McLeod and waited to be greeted.

CHAPTER FIVE

THE RIDE TO Mackenzie Keep took an entire day and part of the next. Tristan shifted atop his horse, his body not quite yet fit enough for the long ride. Unlike him, used to long treks, his steed kept a steady pace that made it hard to avoid being continuously jostled.

"Would ye like for us to stop?" Ruari came alongside, concern etched on his face.

"Nay," Tristan snapped, his gaze stubbornly ahead.

Stopping more than twice would make the trip longer and extend the discomfort, so he focused on the task ahead.

The Mackenzie had some sort of agenda that would eventually benefit the man in some way. The strong clan did not need more lands or warriors. However, gaining either would bring more power, something Laird Mackenzie seemed to treasure.

As Tristan's party continued, a family traveling along the same road blocked their progress. The trudge of a donkey pulling a ragged cart in which a woman and two children rode was excruciatingly slow. A man walked alongside the animal, his hand on its back as if coaxing the tired animal.

"Move to the side!" Tristan called out and one of the children began to cry.

The man turned to him. "There isn't room, sir."

"Make room," Tristan replied.

Somehow, the man managed to move the cart and donkey enough to the side that Tristan and his party could pass. The older child watched them with wide eyes, while the younger cowered into its mother's chest.

The man lifted his gaze to Tristan and shook his head, but didn't utter a word at noting the heavily-armed man and contingent of guards.

Tristan and his party continued past and upon hearing voices, he turned to see one of the guards had dismounted and helped to move the wagon as its wheels had caught in tree roots.

He gritted his teeth. "We do not have time for that."

"Before, ye would have been the one to remain behind and offer assistance," Ruari said when he huffed in annoyance. "We could have managed our way around them."

He searched inside himself in an attempt to find emotion, but only emptiness filled him. There was a time that many things mattered to him, but now, everything was pointless. No use in helping others, when more would take their place. Caring for a friend or lover only meant they'd either betray you or be killed. He'd lost his father and many a friend in the clan wars and now, in all probability, his clan would have to sacrifice more because power-hungry Laird Mackenzie willed it.

"Perhaps I would have, but what good will it do? Wherever that family is headed will only bring them more misery. Some people have such a lot in life."

Tristan motioned forward. "We enter Mackenzie lands."

Ruari looked over his shoulder and held up a fist to get the guards' attention. "Keep vigilant, do not draw yer swords for any reason."

An hour later, they were allowed passage past towering gates into a massive courtyard.

⋙⋘

TRISTAN USUALLY AVOIDED attending politically motivated gatherings and not wishing to be part of the any kind of formal procession, he remained in the courtyard with the guards.

In his opinion, formal entrances were best left to the pompous. On this day, he would not enter and garner a formal welcome from the laird.

Whatever the Mackenzie had to say, he would do so after last meal.

He walked into the stables and upon seeing a man speaking with a woman, cleared his throat.

It was Caylen Mackenzie, whose face lit up at recognizing Tristan. The man didn't say anything else to the woman, choosing to walk back outside with him.

"What brings ye?" Caylen asked after greeting him. He glanced over his shoulder toward the stables. "To interrupt a rather interesting exchange?"

Caylen's roguish reputation was well earned, and he seemed to do his best to keep it intact.

"Yer father's invite." Tristan froze, looking across the way to where McLeod guards gathered. Standing near the stables, his own guardsmen stood as still as statues, also observing. The tension grew when the McLeod guards noticed them.

"There will not be any fighting within our walls," Caylen warned and stalked across the yard to repeat the warning loudly so all the guards could hear.

After a few moments, the men relaxed and began discussing where they'd set up camp, the whole while keeping their eyes on the other group.

Ruari motioned to the far side of the yard, near the stables. "I've spoken with the stable master. He's got room for us. We'll have shelter from the wind and rain."

After a few moments of exchanging annoyed looks with the McLeods, Tristan and his guardsmen carried their bags to the stables and set upon claiming cots.

Unable to prolong it any longer, Tristan went to the front entrance of the home and considered how to enter without making himself too noticeable. It was impossible, of course, given his size. He towered over most men and thanks to the cook's constant insistence that he eat at all hours, Tristan had regained most of his weight.

Upon noticing a side entrance that seemed to allow one into the main house, Tristan turned away from the main entrance and went around a small garden to go in through the narrow door. Once inside, he walked down a long corridor.

There was much activity in the kitchens as he walked by, so he was not noticed as he proceeded toward the sounds in the great room.

Suddenly, someone ran into him from behind. By the light exclamation, he knew it was a woman. Surely someone coming from the kitchens had not expected him to be there. He flattened against the wall to allow whoever it was passage.

"Ye? Ye are alive."

The voice was familiar, melodic. Immediately, he looked to see who it was. The Fae from his dreams studied him intently with her eyes wide and her lips parted. Almost as if she expected him to vanish at any second, she reached out slowly with a finger and poked him in the chest.

Unable to formulate what to say, he remained silent, studying her. With a riot of dark red curls that had escaped its pinnings, bright blue eyes and pink lips, she was a most beautiful creature. If not for the fact he held back, he too wanted to reach out and touch her to ensure she wasn't a figment of his imagination.

"Ye were very ill. I didn't think ye'd survive," she said, this time pressing a hand onto his forearm. "How do ye fare?"

Tristan blinked. "I am well recovered. I am alive because ye and yer husband did what ye could to save me."

For a moment, she frowned at his words and then shrugged and her lips curved. "I am glad. Ye must be very strong to have healed so well."

"I am still not as strong as before," he replied, knowing that despite gaining weight, he was still not as she had seen him.

"Battles do little good. I am thankful there is a truce now."

"Aye," Tristan replied, not quite agreeing, but deciding it was best not to discuss such things with a woman. "Thank ye."

"What is yer name?" she asked.

There was bustling from the direction of the kitchen and several maids hurried toward them with heavily-laden trays. "Hot food!" one announced the obvious.

The red-haired beauty gave him one last smile and hurried away.

He waited for the women with trays to move past and then followed them to the great room. He was more interested now in finding out who the beauty's husband was and whether or not the man deserved such a treasure. In his opinion, any man would be lacking, but he hoped at least she was well treated. From what he remembered, the man had sounded older. It was possible she'd been married off to an established man for her clan's gain.

Upon spotting Laird McLeod, all thought of the woman left and, instead, anger surged that his own father could not be present because of that man's son.

Somehow, his cousin had managed to find a table where they'd sit along a back wall. Tristan hurried there, the entire time scanning the room for a specific man. Although they'd been warned against any type of aggression within the Mackenzie walls, nothing would stop him from killing Ethan McLeod if he was present.

"I do not see him here," Ruari said, knowing who Tristan sought. "If he is here, the bastard remains hidden."

Food was placed in front of him, but Tristan had little appetite, his aching body protesting after the long travel. However, he would eat his fill because it was necessary.

Laird Mackenzie sat upon the high board. With him sat Lady Mackenzie, three sons, which included Caylen, and a woman Tristan did not know. Two men also sat at the high board, probably advisors. The laird had two daughters, both not yet marrying age and they were not present.

Once Tristan began to eat, he relaxed somewhat although it was impossible to let his guard down. Not only were the McLeods in the same room, but there was also the matter of what, exactly, the Mackenzie had in mind.

Everyone lingered after the meal. For what seemed like endless hours, the people continued walking up to the high board and taking the laird's attention for whatever reason they considered important.

Tristan huffed out with exasperation and looked for Ruari, who'd gone out for fresh air.

Deciding it was best to seek out his own guards, he made his way to the front entrance.

Outside, the air was cold. Spring was not in full bloom yet and the winter wind was slow to depart. He'd left his heavier tartan with his other things where he'd be sleeping, so he headed there.

Lanterns lit the way and although it was dark, he could see well enough. On his guard in case of any McLeod decided he should join his father, Tristan maintained high vigil.

The side room to the stables smelled of hay and horse, but was otherwise warm and suitable for sleeping.

"Stop it! I will not stand for yer acting in such a manner," a female voice rang out from a nearby stall. "Duin, I mean it."

If the woman was having a tryst, she didn't sound pleased in the least. "Ouch," she exclaimed. "Be still."

Curious at such a strange conversation and not hearing a man's voice, he opened the door to where the horses were kept and peered in.

"Duin, ye are hateful at times. Poor Fergus will not feed ye after the nip to his hand."

Whoever it was spoke to a horse. The softness of her voice immediately reminded him of the lass who cared for him when he'd been deathly injured. "Merida?"

There was a gasp. A pair of hands appeared at a stall door followed by red hair and, lastly, blue eyes. "Oh, it is ye again." Her brows lowered in a frown. "How do ye know my name?"

"I heard yer husband say it when I was injured."

"Ah." She shook her head. "He is not…"

"Lady Merida," the stable master said as he entered. He looked to Tristan and then to Merida. "I would have looked after Duin. His spitefulness will not dissuade me."

Merida laughed. "He is a spiteful creature."

Just then, a round woman entered the stables, cheeks flushed. "Tis a long time since I have seen ye, lass." She went to Merida and hugged her. "Fergus tells me ye're not married yet."

Fergus was obviously the stable master and the woman who'd entered his wife.

The woman looked to Tristan. "Well, I'll be, here is a suitable husband."

"No," Merida began. "He is not to be my husband, Anne, he is…"

"Nonsense," the woman interrupted. "I sense it. Ye two will be husband and wife." She wagged a finger. "Mark my words."

With a firm nod as if settling things, she turned to her husband. "Come and eat, Fergus. Let these young two people be alone to discuss things."

"Older people and their sensing of things," Merida said, her cheeks a bright red.

Tristan nodded. "Besides, ye are already married, are ye not?"

A slight frown marred her brow. "Ye are referring to Grier, the man in whose cottage ye were. He is not my husband. Grier is a monk, a healer."

There was a light twinge in his chest. Relief perhaps? Of course, there was absolutely no reason for him to feel any sort of reaction at the information.

"And ye?" Merida asked, her gaze pinning him. "Are ye betrothed or married?"

"No reason for it. I am in the middle of clan battles and have no use for a woman in my life at the moment."

"Women are not some sort of tool to be used." Merida's upper lip curled in distaste. "If that is how ye feel, it's no wonder ye are alone."

Not that he needed to explain, so he shrugged. "A distraction. An inconvenience then."

Her lips parted and her eyes narrowed. "Is that what I was when I found ye almost dead and helped drag ye to Grier's cottage then?"

"I…no, of course not."

"Hmmm," she murmured, then turned to the horse. "I know yer problem, Duin. Ye are of the male species. A bother, every single one of ye." Merida gave Tristan one more disapproving look then turned on her heel and hurried away.

Tristan waited a few beats, enjoying the silence of the stables. It was probably the only time he'd have some quiet.

Duin, Merida's horse, watched him with a wary gaze of an animal that didn't trust easily. "I will not touch ye." Tristan felt silly speaking to the animal but, if he were to be truthful, he often spoke to his own.

Hopefully, whatever the Mackenzie wanted could easily be done and they could leave. Tristan let out a long sigh and walked back into the adjoining room to get his tartan. Once it was over his shoulder, he took his time walking back to the house.

"There ye are. The Mackenzie has requested ye come to a room over there." Ruari pointed to a set of doors on the far side of the great room. "I did not see who else went in, but not many, I can tell ye that."

"Come with me," Tristan said. He would not allow the Mackenzie to bring him into a room without at least one guard. His clan was at war, the truce only tentative, so he knew better than to take any kind of chance.

Upon entering, the first thing that took Tristan's attention was the huge table at the center of the room. Around the long table were chairs, three on each side. On one wall was a huge fireplace in which a fire burned, the heat emanating from it enough to dispel the chill from the well-sized room. On one side of the table sat the McLeod, at his side a man he didn't recognize. On the other side were two men, one he recognized as brother to Laird Robertson, a smallish clan nearby. With the Mackenzie sat Caylen, who motioned for him and Ruari to empty chairs opposite the McLeods. No one seemed to be particularly wary, which made Tristan wonder if perhaps some conversation had already taken place before his arrival.

"Welcome, Tristan. How fares yer brother?" the Mackenzie asked without preamble.

"Well," Tristan replied. "He sends his regards."

The Mackenzie nodded. "And the reason for his absence?"

This was a delicate subject that Tristan knew would affect relations between the clans. "He remains behind as burdens of our clanspeople are heavy at the moment. As ye are well aware, the end of winter brings many a problem."

The Mackenzie nodded, seeming, at least on the outside, appeased. "And ye Ruari? I have not seen ye in many years."

Ruari's clear voice seemed to boom in the room. "I come as a representative of Clan Ross to provide any assistance necessary."

It wasn't clear who his cousin meant, exactly. But the fact was that, together, the Ross cousins presented a formidable pair, in stature, physique and reputation as fierce warriors. It was enough of a warning to most: they were not to be toyed with.

"Very well," the Mackenzie began. "I called ye," he looked to the McLeod and then to Tristan, "because I am concerned about the ongoing war between yer clans. The Robertsons as well as Clan Burns, who have nothing to do with this, have been affected. Many of their people have been killed or injured. There are other neighboring villages that have also suffered from this war of yers. Neither of yer clans has taken care to maintain the conflict within yer borders."

Tristan was surprised at the Mackenzie's concerns. Surely, this had more to do than just the clans that came to seek help.

Across the table, the McLeod met his gaze for a moment. There was neither animosity nor friendship, more of an acknowledgement.

The McLeod looked to the Mackenzie. "I can only speak for my men when I say that they were ordered to remain within the boundaries of our territory. Most battles have been fought on our lands, as the Ross are the aggressors."

Since it was true, Tristan let it go. Instead, he focused on a different tactic. "It makes little sense that our warriors would trespass either Robertson or Burns land. They are both north of our lands. Battles have been primarily on the central borders."

"That is not true," the man sitting beside the McLeod replied. "The last attack, led by yer younger brother, was indeed on the north." The man gave him a triumphant lift of his chin. "I would venture to guess on Burns' land."

Tristan leaned forward. "How would we attack if yer men were not there already?"

The Mackenzie cleared his throat and blew out an exaggerated breath. "Ye will come to a truce and end this senseless battling."

"Ethan McLeod killed my father. I doubt yer son would sit idly by if it happened to ye." Tristan speared Caylen with a pointed look. "Would ye?"

Caylen shook his head. "I would not."

"Vengeance has been served, there have been many deaths on both sides." The Mackenzie sat back as if things were settled.

It was laughable that one of the most ruthless men he knew would intervene in this because of two small clans' complaints. However, he knew both the smaller Robertson and the Burns fell under his protection.

The Mackenzie no doubt hoped to maintain a good relationship with the larger Robertson Clan on the eastern region. It was as powerful as the Mackenzie Clan.

Tristan had been instructed what to say and he would not go against Malcolm's and Uncle Gregor's dictates. "I represent Laird Ross, my brother, and his position is that we will not rest until Ethan McLeod pays for what he did. We will not seek out a battle, but we will continue in our quest to find him."

The McLeod stiffened at this and his lips pressed together in a tight line before he spoke. "Ye will not kill my son. Expect us to protect not just him, but all of our people."

The debate would not end for hours, so Tristan looked to a servant who stood nearby. "Ale."

CHAPTER SIX

MERIDA, HER MOTHER and Paige, her brother's wife, were invited to Lady Mackenzie's sitting room. Six women were already seated when they walked in. Some of the women Merida knew, others were strangers. Everyone was animated, excited at the first gathering since the thaw of winter.

Her mother pulled her and Paige through the room, introducing Paige as Alec's wife and managing to drop hints about Merida's need for a husband.

Finally, they were seated in a conversation area with several chairs and tables. Servants brought mead and sweet cakes and the women continued conversing.

Paige seemed content, her eager expression endearing, and Merida couldn't help but take her new sister's hand and squeeze it between her own. "Ye are a dear. Ye make this entire thing bearable."

"Tis something I have yet to believe is happening to me," Paige replied, her eyes bright. "That yer family has accepted me so easily."

Paige was fair, with blonde hair that cooperated much better than Merida's own. She was slender and graceful, seeming more regal than the village girl she'd been raised.

Lady Mackenzie studied Merida for a moment. "I find it surprising that ye have no suitors."

"Tis not for lack of interest," her mother interjected. "Our Merida has been ensconced in our keep for most of the last two years. Her search for a match has been interrupted by the terrifying events of late."

"Yes, of course," Lady Mackenzie replied. "The battles of men affect everyone." She smiled sweetly at Merida, "I am sure we will find ye a suitable husband."

"I do not..." Merida began, but her mother interrupted.

"What my daughter means to say is that we do not wish to be too forward but would be delighted if ye intervened on her behalf to yer husband."

Paige gave Merida a supportive look. Of course, neither would contradict her mother, especially as the nearest group of women, which included Lady Robertson, made no pretense they were not listening in on the conversation.

"My daughter, Lilith, seeks a husband as well," Lady Robertson said, dismissing Merida.

"There ye see, Mother. There are other women seeking help in finding a husband. We cannot expect Lady Mackenzie to make an exception for us."

Lady Mackenzie, who'd stood to speak to a servant, returned to her seat, alight with expectation. "I have the most brilliant idea. Once I speak to my husband, I foresee wonderful news for both Merida McLeod and Lilith Robertson tomorrow. Please know that ye are invited to remain here for at least a few more days." She gave Merida a pointed look, scanning over her hair.

Hopefully, the woman disapproved of her disheveled look enough not to speak on her behalf.

The fact her single status was announced so openly was already bothersome. If the woman planned some sort of celebration, it could mean prolonging their departure for another week. The longer they remained, the higher the chances were that her father would secure a husband for her.

"Mother, I do not want to remain here longer than necessary," Merida mumbled under her breath.

Unfortunately, her mother seemed delighted at Lady Mackenzie's idea. "Are ye not tired of remaining cloistered all winter? This is a good opportunity for ye to find a husband and for making new acquaintances." She then looked to Paige. "Ye as well. Alec will be laird one day and tis good for ye to be friends with other lairds' wives."

Paige paled. The poor young woman was out of her element, unsure of every word she uttered and every action. Although she and her mother had spent the bulk of the winter training with Paige, instructing her on the role she was about to take, it was nothing like the real thing. Now, both she and Paige found themselves on display at the home of the Mackenzies, the largest clan in the region.

Taking pity on Paige, Merida took her arm. "Mother, I think Paige and I will go for a short walk in the garden. I need fresh air."

Before her mother, or anyone for that matter, could protest, they hurried out of the room, practically sprinting to the door and down the stairwell.

The night air was colder than they expected and it took both their breaths away. But that did not deter them from pulling their shawls tightly around their shoulders as they made their way to a small walled side garden where the women had congregated earlier.

"As a child, I remember thinking this garden was huge and magical," Merida said, smiling up at the night sky. "Now it's like any other garden."

Paige came alongside her and also peered up. "I am not sure this is where I should be. I prefer to return home."

"I do as well," Merida said.

"Ye have to accept that this is yer life now." She pointed to the keep. Noting Paige studying the structure, she rubbed the woman's shoulder. "Alongside my brother, ye will make a wonderful laird's wife one day."

When Paige didn't look convinced, Merida touched shoulders with her. "Could ye give up my brother that easily?" Knowing the answer, she hid a smile when Paige sighed.

"Nay, I love him more than life itself," Paige whispered.

"Well, then ye must stop being silly and enjoy this time. For when ye return home, both of ye will be anxious to be alone."

Paige gasped and both of them giggled.

As if he had been beckoned, her brother appeared from around the corner and called for his wife. No doubt, he looked for some time alone, so Merida didn't follow. The sun was low on the horizon, shadows growing longer and larger over the landscape. It was a perfect time for lovers to steal away and get privacy within the gardens or the loch shore nearby.

The coo of a lone bird sounded and Merida listened to the lonely sound and wondered why the wee creature was alone. There was rustling nearby and she decided it was best to go inside and not accidently happen upon a couple intent on spending time alone and not being discovered.

"Surely ye come with a desire to be with me, else ye would not be here," a young woman said in a tone that left no room to wonder what she hoped would happen.

"I do find ye alluring, lass, but I do not seek entanglements," the familiar voice replied.

Merida's eyes widened at hearing Tristan Ross' voice. Somehow, she had to figure out a way to sneak past them.

"Entanglement?" the girl asked, seeming to be taken aback. "Tis that what ye think I wish for?"

Of course it's what she wanted, Merida thought, rolling her eyes.

"I wish ye a good night," Tristan replied and Merida waited to hear what the woman would say next.

There were silence and Merida looked around a young sapling to see what was happening.

By the outlines, it was easy to tell who was who. A young woman leaned forward, her hands on Tristan's chest. She looked up at him, her chin hitched.

"Do not toy with me, Tristan Ross, I can inform my father ye made advancements and he will insist ye marry me." The girl's tone was becoming harsh. "Why else are ye out here?"

Merida took several steps backward and let out a loud sigh. "Tristan," she hissed out as if attempting to whisper. "Are ye here?"

Pretending not to notice the couple that'd now stepped apart, she made a soft sound as if calling a dog. "Tristan?"

"I am here," he replied in a confused tone. "Merida?"

"This is insulting!" His young pursuant huffed and walked a short distance away.

"Ah, there ye are." Merida made a play of hurrying toward him as the young woman had stopped to see what would happen next. She took his rough hand and tugged him back to where she and Paige had been. There was a bench that would hide them from the young woman's view. "Sit."

Although he frowned down at her once Merida sat, he lowered next to her and let out a breath as if relieved. "Had we agreed to meet here?"

"Mother says men are simple beings. I am beginning to understand what she means."

He cocked his head and narrowed his eyes. "Why are ye out here?"

"I am on a rescue mission it seems. First Paige, who needed desperately to leave the women's sitting room. Now I rescued ye from an overly zealous, pampered girl."

His gaze flattened. "I did not require rescuing." When he looked in the direction where the girl had gone, Merida fought not to grin.

"I am so very sorry for the intrusion. I see now. It was a game between ye." She jumped to her feet. "I will retrieve her and explain my actions were one sided."

His hand shot out and took her by the wrist, yanking her none-so-gently to sit again. "Nay, tis not necessary. I have no desire to bed a lass that is barely out of nappies."

"Very well," Merida said, suddenly fully aware she was alone with a warrior, in the middle of the garden, hidden from view. Unsure what to do, she decided it was best to discuss his health. "Have yer wounds fully healed?"

"Aye."

"Good." She fiddled with her skirt. "Perhaps it is safe to leave the garden now."

"Why are ye here at the Mackenzies'?" Tristan asked, once again taking her wrist to ensure she didn't flee. "Tis a talk between lairds about war. Tis no place for a lass like yerself."

She wondered how much to reveal and decided it didn't matter. The reason for her being there would be exposed sooner or later and she preferred to tell Tristan like this, one-on-one.

"My parents hope to marry me to a Mackenzie."

He nodded. "I am surprised to find ye not betrothed as yet. Ye are a beautiful woman."

His compliment took her aback. Tristan Ross did not seem the type to pay compliments. He appeared to be a man used to women approaching him. Merida was willing to bet he rarely had to pursue a woman. Yet she smiled, liking that he did compliment her.

"Thank ye. My parents have been rather patient with me, allowing me freedom for as long as possible."

Tristan nodded. She studied his face for a moment. He was handsome, however not in a classic sense. His nose had been broken before, probably in battle. With cropped hair and a light feathering of a beard, the warrior was alluring. She knew his body, it was formidable although scarred.

It occurred to Merida that she'd yet to reveal her identity and, at the realization, she shivered. "I remember ye, from when yer father visited mine."

"Ye must be cold." For the moment, Tristan seemed to have his mind elsewhere and didn't ask about her clan and she was thankful for it. Suddenly, she needed to get away. First, he was a warrior. At the knowledge that she was sister to the man who'd killed his father, there was no way to know his reaction.

"I best go." She tugged her hand free from his grasp and stood. "I expect we will see each other at morning fast."

He nodded and stood as well. "Where do I know ye from? Ye do look familiar now that I think about it." He studied her. "I am curious…" he began, but she interrupted, pointing at the sky.

"There, did ye see it?"

Following her line of vision, he watched as several stars fell from the sky, leaving a trail of light as they moved.

"Tis magical, are they not?" Suddenly forgetting her plan to escape, Merida continued to watch the sky in case another star would do the same.

"Ye are more interesting to me than the stars." Tristan took her chin and turned her face toward his. Then without warning, he kissed her fully and firmly on the mouth.

A more perfect kiss, Merida would have never imagined. His lips remained atop hers, not demanding but, at the same time, tasting her mouth in a way that made her want to press against him.

Just as she was about to make a fool of herself by allowing her body to fall toward him, Tristan lifted his head and motioned with one arm toward the keep.

"Shall we?"

ALTHOUGH TRISTAN WAS not interested in pursuing a woman at that particular time, he considered who, exactly, Merida was. He went through the clans his family had visited with regularly and tried to remember all the daughters.

For the most part, he attended the meals and then either hunted or competed with other men. Most times, the lairds' wives and daughters were inside during the day. In the evenings, he and the other young men would go about flirting and dancing with the younger lasses if possible.

There were a number of redheads, but he did not recall one as beautiful as Merida.

Perhaps she'd blossomed late.

CHAPTER SEVEN

THE NEXT DAY, Tristan, Ruari and the McLeod were the only ones present in the Mackenzie's study. The air was tense. Without the buffer of the other two clans, they had no choice but to acknowledge each other.

Additionally, it went without saying that Tristan would be the one to decide on the terms of their truce. That was because his clan was stronger and also the aggressors.

"What say ye?" the Mackenzie asked without preamble, his keen gaze trained on Tristan.

Tristan studied the powerful laird. Although he maintained the air of a warrior, by his girth, it was obvious it had been a long time since he'd last seen battle.

"We stand by the temporary truce and will not engage in battle unless provoked." Tristan pinpointed the McLeod with a steady look. "Know that yer son will not be able to hide forever." He then looked back to the Mackenzie. "Our father's death is not fully avenged until Ethan McLeod is dead."

The McLeod started to speak, but the Mackenzie held up his hand to silence him. "Tis what I expected. My wife brought to me a suggestion that may be a way to help gain peace between yer clans."

A trickle of apprehension traveled down Tristan's spine. And by the way the McLeod stiffened and his eyes narrowed, the man didn't know what the Mackenzie was about to say either.

"Yer daughter is here to seek a husband," the Mackenzie said to McLeod who nodded and seemed to relax, but frowned. "What has that to do with…" He left the sentence hanging, his wide eyes going to Tristan.

When Ruari sat up straighter, his eyes narrowing, Tristan placed a hand on his cousin's forearm to ensure he didn't say something inappropriate.

Tristan shook his head. Truce in the balance or not, he was not about to marry a McLeod, probably a spoiled girl, like the one from the night before. "I am not here to find a wife. I am here to represent my brother."

As if he'd not spoken, the Mackenzie continued. "A marriage between the clans would suit everyone's purposes."

Not to be dissuaded, Tristan groaned. "How exactly would it benefit my clan?" he said between clenched teeth.

"Ye would be in good standing with mine," Laird Mackenzie replied. "And…ye would gain an alliance with the McLeods, the Burns' and, of course, the Robertsons."

None of it mattered to his clan. Tristan, however, was not about to argue with the Mackenzie. "As this is an unexpected request, I must send a messenger to my brother."

The McLeod leaned forward, hands flat on the table surface. "I do not wish to use my daughter as a pawn. Although I did come seeking a husband for her, I would have preferred to join with yer clan, not the Ross'."

The Mackenzie nodded. "Tis understandable. However, tis imperative that I protect my clan and alliances and this is a way for ye to be part of it."

There would be no arguing with the powerful man, but Tristan hoped that by gaining time, he could come up with a way not to have to marry. He'd not considered marriage. Although many times in bed one lass or another had intrigued him, it wasn't until lately that any woman truly piqued his interest.

The healer, Merida, would be the only woman he'd even consider. She was probably the daughter of one of the visiting clans. Tristan wondered which. Perhaps it was time to find out.

"Can we wait until I get word from my brother before I reply?" Tristan asked, expecting the Mackenzie to rebuff his request.

As predicted, the man pressed his lips together in disapproval. "Ye may let him know and invite him to be present for the marriage ceremony." The man rose to his full height, which was not as tall as Tristan. Nonetheless, he exuded power.

"Let me make things clear," the Mackenzie said as he looked to Tristan and then to the McLeod. "I strongly suggest a marriage between Tristan Ross and yer daughter. Either both of ye do as I say or talks are over and ye both will be considered my enemies."

The words hung in the thick air.

First to respond, the McLeod nodded and spoke in a flat tone. "I will abide by yer wishes, Laird. My daughter will be prepared."

The Mackenzie's cool gaze slid to Tristan.

He let out a breath. "Very well. Ye have my word, I will marry the McLeod's daughter." Tristan met the McLeod's gaze. The man had been friendly with his father. They had hunted and competed against one another during their youths. Admittedly, Tristan liked the McLeod and had grown to respect him over the years. It was the actions of Ethan McLeod that had made them enemies.

"I vow to be a good husband to yer daughter."

He tried to remember the McLeod's daughter. The only time he'd seen her, it was perhaps ten years earlier. The chit had been a plain, red-haired, freckle-faced lass that often trailed after them on a huge horse. Her skinny legs pressed tightly against the animal formed a comical sight.

He groaned inwardly at the memory. It would take a miracle for her to have transformed into anything lovely.

"Thank ye," the McLeod replied.

Immediately, the Mackenzie's countenance changed and a broad grin formed. "Good," he exclaimed and clapped his hands together. "Let us toast. Allow three days for preparations."

After several more minutes of listening to what all had to be done, Tristan and Ruari walked out to the courtyard.

They joined the guards who were relaxing under some trees. He wasn't sure what to think of the events transpiring. Things were out of his control.

Upon seeing him, a guard got to his feet. "Can we leave now?" His eyes narrowed. "Why the glum faces?"

"I must send one of ye to get an urgent message to my brother." Tristan looked around to ensure they were out of earshot. He motioned to the guards to form a circle. "The Mackenzie wishes me to marry the McLeod's daughter."

Every set of eyes rounded. Ruari spit on the ground. "How did this come to be?"

"The grumbling of the lesser clans supposedly." Tristan waved a hand impatiently. "I believe it is the Mackenzie proving how strong he is against everyone. I do not believe he cares one way or another about the small clans. Tis a show of power, nothing else."

"Lower yer voice," Ruari whispered, looking past him. "We do not need more trouble."

When he released a breath, it was as if Tristan had been holding it for too long. He looked over his shoulder and noticed the McLeod's guards were studying them with curiosity. "They must have heard," he muttered.

"How is this going to work?" Ruari asked. "We cannot be joined with them. What about Ethan?"

"Have no doubt," Tristan hissed into his cousin's ear. "That coward will die. Neither truce nor marriage will keep him safe. I told them both in the room that we would not stop seeking our vengeance."

One of the guards cleared his throat, the lanky young guard named Gavin. He often served as scout or messenger because of his steed's speed. "I will go back. What would ye like me to say?"

"Tell my brother that I am being directed to marry the McLeod's daughter and not given a choice by the Mackenzie. It is set to happen in three days. Tell him the McLeod has agreed and so have I."

The young man nodded. "I'll go now. Do not worry, I will be there by morning."

"Be with care," Tristan said, knowing Gavin sometimes pushed himself too far. "Do not return. Allow someone else to take yer place."

There wasn't much to do, so Tristan decided to relax on his cot for a few hours and ignore the goings-on. He needed time to process what had occurred and get used to the idea that in three days he would be a married man.

"Will ye bring her to the keep? Do ye think they will insist on visiting her?" Ruari walked behind him to the rooms beside the stables.

Tristan gave up on the idea of time alone when the usually quiet Ruari sat on the next bed and stared at him as if expecting some sort of interesting reaction. "At least she's comely," he remarked in a quiet voice.

"Who?" Tristan raked his fingers down his face. "Whom do ye speak of?"

"The McLeod's daughter. She's quite lovely."

Tristan wasn't sure he was ready to hear more about the woman he was to be tied to. However, he was curious. "Have ye met her?"

"Tristan Ross. My laird wants to speak to ye alone," said a guard standing at the doorway.

"God's foot, what now?" Tristan grumbled to no one in particular and stood.

The Mackenzie was on the far side, away from the center of the courtyard, watching his guardsmen spar. Tristan wanted to roll his eyes. If the man spent more time practicing than just watching swordplay, perhaps he'd have less time to manipulate other people's lives.

"Laird," Tristan said, meeting the Mackenzie's gaze before looking to a pair of huge warriors that seemed to be out for blood.

The Mackenzie motioned to the men who fought. "Seems one of them is not too keen on the other having slept with his wife."

When one of the warriors sliced across, cutting the arm of his opponent, the Mackenzie turned away as if bored. "An alliance between our clans would bring yers power. No one would dare make an attempt on yer brother's life."

"Do ye mean an alliance or my clan falling under yer control?" Tristan replied, ensuring to keep his tone even. "We are in alliance with the Sutherland and the Munro." He wanted to add that, together, they were as large as Clan Mackenzie.

"Alliances rise and fall. However, by this marriage, yer clan will gain the McLeod's alliance."

Tristan was no fool and kept his mouth shut. Whatever the Mackenzie wanted to say, it was best to hear it.

"The McLeod has not called upon the larger McLeods. Did ye ever wonder why?"

"It's not for me to know. Our qualm is with Ethan McLeod."

A loud growl sounded as one of the fighters thrust his sword into the side of the other. The man screamed, but found the strength to strike back, sending his opponent stumbling backward.

Tristan glanced past the fighters to the guards who watched. At this point, it was hard to tell if they took sides.

When both fighters stalled, attempting to catch their breaths, the Mackenzie signaled for guards to intervene and break up the sword match. At this point, Tristan wondered if either man would survive their wounds. Both bled profusely, one falling flat on his face into the ground.

"Ye may have lost two seasoned warriors," Tristan said as the men were dragged way.

"I lost them when they began this feud. They would have probably turned against each other anyway."

The lack of care and compassion in the Mackenzie's countenance reminded him of his own brother. Malcolm never wavered, not in battle and not when seeing his men die. It was as if Malcolm's soul left his body the day their father died.

Now that he was married to a woman named Elspeth, he did seem to have regained some of his humanity. And yet, he would never be the same Malcolm as before.

Tristan couldn't help but wonder if his own marriage would change him.

He cared little for his enemies. Whether they were cut down, drowned or hanged, no option would bother Tristan in the least. War hardened a man. Like a thief in the night, it stole any desire to help others, or to be any kind of savior.

Had the Mackenzie expected him to intervene, to ask the fight to be stopped? Tristan hadn't considered asking for intervention. If the warriors ended up dead, it was because they chose to fight of their own accord.

The Mackenzie hesitated, his calculating gaze moving over Tristan. "I heard ye were close to death. Now ye are to be married to a lovely lass. Makes one wonder, does it not?"

"Exactly what?" Tristan had to admit he'd not considered the reason for fate bringing him to where he stood now. "Tis not my wish to be married right now. I wish to avenge my father's death. However, I do realize tis best for my clan that the war with the McLeod ceases."

"But ye will continue to hunt down his son." The Mackenzie made the statement matter-of-factly. "He is here."

Tristan's eyes widened. "Here?" he repeated, unsure what to do next. "Where?"

The Mackenzie shrugged. "Probably being sent away. If it were my son, I would not have allowed him to be here in the first place."

"It matters not," Tristan spat out, his gaze scanning the entire area. "He will not live much longer."

"Killing the McLeod's son here would bring consequences for yer clan. I will not stand idly by and allow my people to be in danger."

Since when. Tristan bit down with force to keep from uttering the words.

"I will marry the lass if ye insist on it. I have given my word. However, be clear, Laird, this will not make my clan friends of the McLeod."

"Just family," the Mackenzie replied with a chuckle. "Sometimes that can be worse I suppose."

Tristan stopped the man before he could walk away. "Why did the McLeod not call upon the larger clan for help?"

"Because his son has made enemies of them as well. I believe he maimed a cousin, the first born of the McLeods of the east, during sword practice."

Chapter Eight

Clyde McLeod rushed into the dim chamber and directly to the bed. He pulled back the bedding that covered two nude people.

"Get out," he hissed to a young woman who gasped and hurried from the bed. He didn't wait for her to finish dressing, but took her by the arm and pulled her to the door. "Finish dressing in the hallway." He shoved her outside and closed the door on the startled woman.

Unlike the woman, the young man in bed sat up, his back on the pillows and gave Clyde a bored look. "What are ye doing, Father? Ye directed me to not leave the chamber and now ye take my company?"

Anger surged at how nothing concerned Ethan. If he feared death, it was not evident. It was almost as if he'd lost any care or perhaps he'd never had it to begin with.

"Ye must leave at once."

"Pray tell, why?" Ethan finally slid from the bed, wrapped a tartan around his waist and went to the small window. "Is there something happening ye wish me to not know about?"

Although rash and without thought, Ethan was not stupid. His keen eyes met his father's. "What have ye done now?"

In two steps, Clyde was nose to nose with his youngest. "Tis what ye did that I must continue to contend with. Yer actions have cost us much again. Now we lose yer sister to the scheming of the Mackenzie."

"It is time for her to be married off. Best that we acquire something for it. I do not see why it upsets ye."

Knowing it was best that Ethan not know exactly who Merida was to marry, Clyde huffed and turned away. "Get dressed and prepare to leave. Go back to our home and gather guards to check our northern borders."

Ethan looked back out the window. "Sending me away will not keep me from finding out what happens." He turned back to this father. "I do not care one way or another, Father. If Merida marries, if ye send people to war without me, it matters naught to me."

When Clyde placed a hand on Ethan's shoulder, the younger man frowned. "Ethan, is there anything ye do care about? Do ye ever wish for anything?"

"Nay, tis all futile. Life is not worth more than the moment. A tryst with a woman brings temporary pleasure. Eating a tasty food morsel the same. However, nothing brings greater pleasure than control over another human. That moment when ye can be the one to decide whether they live or die."

"Pleasure is not the same thing as happiness, nor is it joy. What ye speak of are all temporary." Clyde studied Ethan for a long moment.

"Ye should remain at our watch post to the north. It would avoid more trouble for our clan. Do something for the good of the clan for a change, Ethan."

Ethan shrugged from under his father's hand and stalked to the bed. "I will leave with haste, ensuring not to be seen."

"Go north and stay there."

His face twisted in anger, Ethan closed the distance between them until they were nose to nose. "Do not command me. Ye have no right. Never once have ye cared about what I say or do. Why start now?"

"That is not true," Clyde replied, his jaw tense. "Ye just refused any kind of caring. I don't understand ye. But know this Ethan, my son or not, I will not stand for ye to bring more death to the clan."

Ethan took a step back, his expression murderous. "I will do as I please."

For a long moment, Clyde studied his son. How was this young man birthed from the same two parents and was so very different than the fair and just Alec, or the kind and caring Merida?

"If ye do, do not expect our clan to protect ye."

Ethan snorted. "Ye have no choice."

"Do not push me on this, Son."

When Ethan stalked to the side of the room and lifted up his burlap bag, it was clear the conversation was over. "Await until ye are informed it is clear before leaving."

THE NEXT EVENING at last meal, Merida joined her mother at a table near the front of the great room. The meal was simple; cheeses, roasted goat meat and fresh bread. Bowls of savory broth with bits of root vegetables were served as well.

The room had been cleaned, fresh rushes spread and although it remained a bit chilly, there were no fires in the hearth. Merida was glad for her shawl and was about to complain about the cool room when she spotted lads hurrying to both hearths with armfuls of chopped wood.

"I think Lady Mackenzie expected a warmer evening," her mother remarked.

Merida nodded and giggled. "The day is warmer than usual, however, tis always a bit colder indoors."

When her father descended the stairs and entered the great room, Merida sensed he was not at ease. By the way her mother studied him, she too noticed something about his countenance that seemed different.

"He is worried about things and the meeting with the Mackenzie may have not gone well." Her mother smiled when he joined them and lowered to sit. "Do ye need something, Husband?" She motioned for a servant to bring him drink.

The girl poured ale into a cup and placed it before Merida's father. "I will bring a platter with meats and cheese," she announced before turning to fill another man's cup.

"I must speak to ye both. Tis of utmost importance."

Merida looked around the room, unsure what to think. There didn't seem to be anything afoot. "Where is Ethan?"

"He's returning home. I have tasked him with ensuring our borders are well secured. Tis time to place guards at the posts."

Her mother leaned close to her father. "Is something dangerous about to happen?"

It was endearing when her father covered her mother's hand. "Nay, do not worry yerself. But with spring here, it means men are out seeking easy prey of unprotected borders and people."

There were not as many people in the great room as the days before. Two of the visiting clans had departed early to return home. There were empty tables where the guards normally ate last meal, which meant they were in all probability eating outdoors.

The Mackenzie stood and motioned to guards, who hurried away.

"What now?" her father grumbled and took a long drink from his cup. He motioned for the same servant girl who immediately refilled it.

Within moments, two sets of guardsmen entered.

From one doorway, a group of Clan Ross men entered, their tartan colors proudly displayed. Merida stiffened upon noting that her own clan guardsmen entered the other side and stood seeming to wait for some sort of announcement.

"What is happening?" her mother asked, her hand clutching her shawl at her chest. "Clyde?"

"I'd hoped to tell ye before, but I must go to my men." He stood and walked to stand before his guards.

At the same time, Tristan Ross went to stand with his men. His expression seemed relaxed, as he kept his gaze to the front of the room. Everyone in the room was silent, as those in attendance waited for whatever was to be said.

The Mackenzie made a show of scanning the room. Merida was shocked when his gaze rested on her for a moment. She let out a breath of relief when he finally looked away.

"As ye may be aware, Clan Ross and Clan McLeod have been at war," the man began and paused for effect. "I brought them both here to bring forth the discussion of a truce."

"We were already in a truce," Merida whispered. Her mother motioned for her to remain silent.

"Part of the agreement is that the clans will be united. And as such, an attack by one or the other, would be an attack on themselves."

Her mother frowned and let out a breath. Merida had to agree to the silent communication. The Mackenzie enjoyed attention a bit too much. His wife, who was looking around the room, seemed just as enthusiastic by the way she leaned forward and had her lips curved in approval.

Lady Mackenzie's gaze traveled over the people gathered as if searching for someone in particular. Upon seeing Merida, her eyes widened and her smile grew wider as if in glee.

"What is she up to?" Merida hissed. "Mother, did she say anything to ye about me?"

A woman sitting across the table looked to her. "Shhh."

"I am pleased to announce that there will be nuptials between Clan Ross and Clan McLeod." Murmurs rose, and heads swiveled from one group to the other. When the people quieted, everyone now enthralled to see what would happen, the Mackenzie motioned with one hand toward Clan Ross.

"Tristan Ross, come forward," the Mackenzie said, hand outstretched. When Tristan walked to the front of the room, he turned and faced the crowd.

His gaze remained forward, his expression blank. Merida looked to her father who stared at the Mackenzie, his jaw set firmly.

What was happening? She couldn't figure out how it was possible that there was a marriage between the clans and she had no idea who was involved. She'd not heard of any of her cousins coming. "Mother..." She stopped speaking at noticing how pale her mother had become.

"Merida McLeod, approach." The Mackenzie's voice felt like a slap and Merida whirled to meet Tristan's widened gaze.

"What?" Merida said, not moving. It wasn't until her mother gave her a light shove that she managed to stand and take a couple steps toward the front.

"Go on, girl," an impatient person said, giving her yet another push.

"I...I am not sure what is happening..." Once again, she looked to her father, who motioned with both hands for her to go forward.

When she came to where Tristan stood, she looked up at him. "Did ye know?"

"Aye."

Crossing her arms over her chest, she glared up at the Mackenzie. "I was not informed of this. I will not be bartered off like a prized cow..."

Before she could continue, strong arms wrapped around her and she was more dragged than guided out a side door.

Behind her, the Mackenzie continued to speak as if nothing had happened. "Through this marriage, peace will descend in the region. Our people will no longer be afraid to traverse past borders to visit family or sell wares..."

"Let me go," Merida shouted. "I must return and ensure that man is aware I am not a puppet to be handed off at will."

Tristan released his embrace, but held her arm. "Tis best ye wait until ye are not so cross."

"Cross! I am not cross!" Merida screamed. "I am furious."

"Merida!" Her mother exited the doorway and hurried over. For a moment, Merida thought she was about to cover her mouth by the way her mother held both hands out. "Lower yer voice at once."

Too angry to think clearly, she would not be mollified. "Did ye know as well?"

"Nay, but we did come seeking ye a husband."

"A husband, aye. One that would be an attribute to our clan. Not a Ross." She turned to Tristan. "I do not mean to offend ye."

"I am not offended," he replied and shrugged.

She studied him for a moment. "Why did ye agree? I know ye and yers detest my clan."

"I was not given a choice, Lady Merida."

Merida lost steam, unsure what to do next. "Surely if ye and my father stood up to the Mackenzie and not allow him to dictate, it would not have happened."

"Wife." Her father stood in the doorway.

He motioned for his wife and then met Merida's gaze. Fury exuded from him. "Ye will remain here until ye accept it. Once ye and yer husband-to-be come to terms, ye will return inside and apologize to our host."

Merida started to respond that she would not, however, she'd never seen her father so angry. He glared at her. "Ye have disgraced us with yer behavior, Merida. Ye act like a child, disrespecting our host."

With that, he took her mother's arm and they went back inside.

Looking to the doorway for longer than needed, Merida suddenly became aware of the large, muscular and extremely handsome man who stood silently and solidly beside her, waiting for what she'd do next.

Tristan Ross was to become her husband.

And yet, she continued to be furious.

CHAPTER NINE

"I DO NOT wish to apologize."

Tristan wasn't sure why, but he wanted to laugh. Merida was so contrite her expression was almost comical.

She'd not seemed to realize they were to be married until the last moment. It seemed her anger was based more on being dictated to than the fact she and he were to become man and wife.

"It cannot be undone. Ye must obey yer father."

When she whirled toward him, he was astounded at how beautiful the woman was when she was angry. Her face flushed and her lip curled, she reminded him of a fabled fury. Darkened blue eyes flashed from the door to him.

"I suppose I will have to obey ye once we marry. From one master to another, such is the life of women."

"A man should not dictate to a wife. One would hope the woman would be intelligent enough to know what should be done and what should be left alone." Tristan took her arm and slowly turned her to face him. He then lifted her chin so their gazes met.

"What do ye think is best right now, Merida McLeod?"

Her brow crinkled as she considered his question. "Tis best I apologize and, after, ask that he grant ye and I time to know each other."

"That would mean remaining here longer. Is that what ye wish?"

"I'd not considered that." Merida covered her cheeks with both hands. "What do ye think?"

"The sooner we marry, the sooner ye and I can return to my home."

Her eyes widened. "Yer home," she said slowly. "I am never returning to mine, am I?"

In an effort to divert her attention, he lowered his mouth and covered hers.

At first, she responded. Merida's body fell forward until against his. Taking full advantage, he wrapped her into his embrace, pulling the fetching woman tightly. He'd been looking to distract her, but had instead succeeded in his own departure from the present because, in that moment, everything disappeared.

One kiss after another, he pressed his lips from her mouth down to the side of her face to just below her ear.

Merida's fingers grasped the thick fabric of his tunic and let out a long sigh. When she pushed him backward, it caught him so off guard that he stumbled. The reality of the moment, the cool wind and surrounding sounds immediately reappeared.

Wide pools of dark blue reminding him of the color of the sky met his. "Why did ye do that?"

"Do what?" Tristan responded with a frown. "Kiss ye?"

"Yes, that. Ye had no right." Her chest lifted and lowered, a flush lifting from her neck to her cheeks. "That was…it was…" She seemed to lose the ability to speak and instead huffed and rolled her eyes.

"It was nice?" He took a step closer. "We will be doing more than kissing once we marry."

"If we do, which I still do not believe will happen." Merida turned away. "I must go see after Duin."

He caught up with her and they walked in silence toward the corrals. "Ye have to apologize to the Mackenzie."

When she let out a second huff, he realized it was her response when she was annoyed. "I know. But I refuse to do it in front of everyone."

"Ye misbehaved in plain view of all those present."

Shoulders rounded, she stopped. "Ye're right. I may as well do it and get it done with."

They returned to the great room. The noise of cups hitting tables, conversations and a fiddler meant she'd have to go close to where the laird sat to be heard. Tristan accompanied her to stand before the laird and await his acknowledgement.

The Mackenzie had daughters so Tristan was reassured when the man looked upon Merida with the indulgent look fathers often gave unruly daughters. "Have ye something to say, lass?"

Merida looked to where her parents sat and nodded. "Aye, Laird. I apologize for my behavior earlier. Ye see, I was caught by surprise." She leaned forward. "Tis not a good idea for me to marry him." She motioned to Tristan with her head. "He is my enemy."

The laird chuckled and met Tristan's gaze. "Ye will nay be bored with yer wife. Treat her well."

"Aye." Tristan wondered how long it would be before Merida accepted that he, a Ross, would not only be her husband, but she would forever now be part of his clan.

AFTER THE MEAL, Tristan offered to go with Merida to see about her horse. Her parents urged her to accept and she trudged alongside him as if being punished.

"I thought ye liked me," Tristan said in an effort to start a conversation. "Or was it just compassion for an injured man?"

She shrugged. "I do like ye. But tis not what worries me about marrying ye." Her gaze swept over him. "Ye are too big."

It took effort not to laugh at her statement. "So it is not my clan that ye object to, but my size?"

As if he were a child, she took his hand and led him until they reached the corrals. "I know what transpires between a husband and wife," Merida whispered. "My friend, Frieda, said tis most unpleasant and that because her husband was large, it was worse."

"I see," Tristan replied. "I assure ye, I have never hurt a woman in that manner. Quite the opposite."

Her eyes narrowed. "Perhaps."

"Come." He guided her to the side of the stables where they would not be seen. "I promise not to hurt ye or take yer maidenhead. But to show ye how it feels."

MERIDA WASN'T SURE why she agreed, but instantly there was a heating sensation between her legs that seemed to present itself whenever she was in close proximity to Tristan.

He pulled her into a dark corner beside the stables, the cramped area blocked off on three sides. Pulling at her skirts, he lifted them up and held them with one hand.

Like earlier, his mouth covered hers and she couldn't help but respond. His kisses brought too many sensations, overwhelming to the point of complete distraction.

However, through the haze, his hand sliding up her inner thigh permeated and she tensed.

"Relax, I will not hurt ye."

Ever so slowly, his fingers moved up and down her thigh, caressing the much too sensitive skin. His actions made every single inch of her body tingle. She wanted more, but when she parted her lips to ask, his tongue slid past.

The invasion was delicious, sending new currents of heat to every part of her being. It was then that his fingers finally found her core. She gasped at the strange sensations.

Tristan slipped a finger down the center of her sex, gently flicking until she lost the ability to stand. Thankfully, he held her upright when her legs quivered. Grasping his tunic, she wished there was more to what happened and at the same time, it had to end else she cry out and bring unneeded attention.

The heat at her center was intense. The combination of his kisses and ministrations so overwhelming that when he slid a finger into her, she dissolved, losing all control.

Thankfully, his mouth over hers and muted any sounds she made. Merida pulled her head away and leaned against his chest. Attempting to control her breath, she gulped before speaking. "Stop. I cannot take more without begging for something I'll regret."

Immediately, his hand was gone and her skirts fell to the ground. He embraced her against his hard chest that heaved with each breath.

They remained in the embrace for a long moment. Merida wanted to ask him questions. What had been the one elusive thing she'd wanted? Why had the world seemed to spin? Instead, she took a breath and looked up to him.

He was magnificent. Too handsome for words and yet at the same time a rugged, seasoned warrior.

"I feel that perhaps the marriage bed will not be as distasteful as Frieda claims."

Tristan's deep chuckle made Merida smile.

MERIDA FLOATED INTO her chambers. It was as if everything had been painted over, the colors around her much more vibrant.

How was it possible for so many new sensations to be just now discovered by her? She'd been convinced men were the only ones who found pleasure in intimacy. If what Tristan had shown her was any indication, there was definitely a great deal of delight a woman felt as well.

As she prepared for bed, the stark reality of what her marriage meant descended like a wet blanket across her shoulders. When she left Mackenzie Keep, she'd be part of Clan Ross. With the animosity between the clans, it meant she'd probably not see her parents or brothers for months on end.

Her new friendship with Paige would end.

Everything she'd known all her life, all the people and surroundings would be gone forever.

When she sniffed, her companion, Elsa, rushed to her. "Are ye scared of what will happen, Lady Merida?" The young woman patted her back. "That man is intimidating."

"I fear not seeing my family. Moving away to live with our enemies."

Elsa sighed and nodded. "I will come with ye."

"Thank ye." Merida hugged the young woman and both began to cry.

Chapter Ten

Paige was awakened by a sound and reached for Alec and found she was alone in bed. Remembering he'd returned to their keep now that all had been settled, she let out a sigh.

Slipping from the bed, she went to the window. She had a view of the courtyard and the gates. Both were as expected for the middle of the night, nothing seemed off. However, there was a troubling tingle in her chest and Paige decided to investigate what was happening.

Donning a shawl over her nightgown, she tiptoed across the room toward the door. Just as she reached the doorway, someone yanked her back and against the wall.

"Ethan?" she whispered. "I thought ye had returned home."

"Why should I?" His breath reeked of ale and she turned her head away.

"What are ye doing in my chambers?" she replied, attempting to pull away, but he held her fast.

"I do not believe my brother would mind sharing ye. We've shared plenty a lass over the years."

A feeling like that of a boulder formed in the pit of her stomach. Paige wondered how to get attention without alerting the entire household.

"Let me go." She did her best to keep her tone even. "Ye are drunk."

His chuckle was dry, without mirth. "Aye, I am. And in need of a woman to fuck."

"If ye do not release me, I will cry out."

"No, ye will not. Tis boring to be with one man and ye want to experience more."

What he said made no sense. Her heart thundered in her chest and an errant tear slipped down her temple. What would she do if this happened? Tell Alec? Her mind raced.

She shoved him backward, but he held fast, much too strong for her. His mouth covered hers. With his body and one hand, he held her still and gripped her breast with his free one.

Paige gagged and scratched his face, but nothing deterred him.

Finally, she lifted her leg and kneed him in the groin. He fell onto the floor cupping both hands between his legs and grunting in pain. "Bitch."

Thinking it best to find his mother, she took a step forward only to stumble back when he grabbed the hem of her nightgown. "I will have ye under me," Ethan said, his voice still hoarse with pain.

Just as she fell forward, Paige grabbed a teapot from a small side table and swung it as hard as she could across Ethan's face. His head lolled to the side and he let out a long breath and went still.

Ethan lay motionless on the floor, his mouth slack. Paige gasped and crawled away. Had she killed him? If so, what would happen to her?

WHEN SOMEONE SHOOK her awake, Merida almost screamed. After a moment, the sleep ebbed. A disheveled Paige loomed over her.

"What is going on?" Merida mumbled, scooting over. "Do ye want to sleep here?"

"No, wake up," Paige hissed, taking her by the shoulders. "Ye must come with me at once."

At the urgency in Paige's voice, Merida was fully awake. "What is wrong?"

Before she could get her bearings, Paige had yanked her from the bed and tugged her out the door. Once they entered Paige's chamber, Merida understood why her brother's wife was so upset.

"I hit him because he tried to…he made advances. He was drunk." Paige had begun to cry now. "Is he dead?"

Merida had witnessed many a time that Ethan had passed out from too much drink. He was breathing, but it was worrisome to see blood trickling from his forehead and down the side of his face. She touched his face, he was cool to the touch, and then felt his neck and shook him.

Whatever he mumbled was incoherent. Ethan batted her away sloppily and turned to his side and let out a long breath.

"I'll get Da. Stay here with him," Merida instructed. "He will not wake."

She hurried out the door and down the hallway, only to stop abruptly upon seeing Tristan.

He, too, stopped and studied her. "Is something wrong?"

Unfortunately, she stood under a torch and he saw the bloodstain on her nightgown. "Are ye injured?"

"I…" Merida looked down at her nightgown. "No, I am fine. Paige is not feeling well. I am going to seek my mother."

Tristan frowned. "There's blood on yer clothing."

"Tis not blood," she lied and prayed he'd not insist that it was, so she quickly added, "tis tincture I made for Paige and spilled some."

Seeming to take her at her word, he nodded and didn't try to stop her as she hurried past.

Inside her parents' chambers, Merida was at a loss who to wake. Her mother would know what to do, but her father should be the one to deal with Ethan. In the end, she shook her father awake.

Together with her parents, they returned to Paige's chamber. Her mother immediately went to comfort Paige and her father yanked Ethan up to sit. "Why are ye still here?" he demanded. "Ye were supposed to return home."

Ethan babbled about not being able to get to his horse and then other things that didn't make sense.

In the end, Merida's mother cleaned up his face and her father half-dragged him to their chamber.

"I will remain with him," her father said as they put Ethan to bed. "Yer mother can go with ye."

Merida studied Ethan in his slumber for a moment. "He tried to take advantage of Paige."

Her mother gasped and glared at the sleeping Ethan. "Something must be done about him." She turned to Merida. "Neither ye nor Paige will say anything to Alec about this. Allow yer father and me to handle it."

"Come now," her mother urged. "Ye must get some sleep. There's just one more day before the wedding."

It was hard to imagine what would happen if Tristan found out Ethan was there. Would their marriage happen if he killed her brother? Probably not. The war would begin again and, this time, the Mackenzie would be involved. She detested how much her brother's stupidity always affected so many. And yet, he slept without a care, like there was absolutely nothing wrong.

"We must by all means keep his being here a secret," her mother whispered when they entered Merida's chamber. "The marriage must take place without anything to stop it. Our clans must have peace despite Ethan's irresponsible actions."

Her mother instructed that she climb into bed with Paige, who remained upset. Then she lay on a pallet of blankets in front of the hearth. A mother guarding her young.

Merida couldn't sleep. Why had Tristan been in the hallway? Did he suspect Ethan was about? It had not helped that he'd bumped into her and seen the bloodstain on her clothing. To start a marriage by lying to her husband was not how she'd have preferred. However, peace and the safety of her clan were of the utmost importance.

Hopefully, her father would enlist a guard's help and get Ethan out of the keep and away before sunrise.

One more day and she'd be married to Tristan Ross. By all accounts, she considered them to be compatible. It was obvious to her that he found her attractive by the way his gaze seemed to constantly follow her movements.

As far as her attraction to him, Tristan had always been on her mind since finding him unconscious in the woods.

Even when not admitting how much she desired him, deep inside, she'd wondered how it would feel to be kissed by him. After their time together by the stables, now she wondered about more. The desire to be intimate and join with him took over other thoughts.

Morning would come and she feared the day ahead. If only Ethan had left.

A ROOSTER'S CROW woke Tristan and he moaned. His throat was dry and his head heavy. He'd drunk too much whisky the night before in Caylen's chambers. Two other men had joined them for a few hours of gaming.

Women had been brought in to entertain, but he'd refrained from participating in it. Soon, he'd be married and foremost on his mind was the idea of the marriage bed with Merida.

His temples pounded and Tristan squeezed his eyes tighter. "Ruari?" he said to the emptiness.

"Too much to drink last night does not excuse ye from helping with the horses." Ruari laughed a bit too loudly.

After getting up, Tristan walked over to a water barrel and dunked his head into the frigid water. It helped to dispel the headache, but only a bit.

He trudged behind Ruari to where their horses were. Thankfully, his cousin took pity and motioned to a crooked chair. "Sit down before ye fall over. I'll see after the horses."

Just few feet away, Merida walked away from the corral, tugging a horse behind her. It wasn't her horse, but a large beast of the same size. She stopped and ran her hand down the animal's nose as if to reassure it. He wondered if it was her father's.

Unlike when she was inside the keep, she seemed more herself outdoors in the company of horses.

Tristan took a deep breath, thankful for the cold air and tried to remember if he'd truly seen her the night before in the corridor in a bloodstained nightgown. He'd been heading away from Caylen's chambers, heading to seek his bed. And although having drank too much, he'd not been so inebriated to not notice her.

He pondered her reply to his question. She'd lied and said it was a tincture. Then again, if it was that she'd been having her womanly courses, it wasn't something she would have readily admitted.

Putting the thought away, he searched for her but she'd gone off with the horse. After a few moments, she reappeared from the direction of the front gates, this time without the horse.

Interesting.

One of his guards neared. The man yawned and scratched at his beard. "Should I ride out to see if yer brother sends word?"

Tristan considered the man and understood. He, too, was becoming restless, too many days behind walls and in the company of enemies no less.

"Aye, good idea. Take several with ye. I have no need of guards here."

"We cannot leave ye unprotected. There are too many McLeods."

Tristan considered the guard's words. "True, take only four with ye."

"Aye, the McLeods are not trustworthy," the guard said.

"A clan to which I will be joined to by marriage tomorrow."

The guard shook his head. "We hope it will not happen." He studied Tristan. "Ye do not wish it either, do ye, Tristan?"

"Nay." He bit the word out. "I would rather not marry, and especially not a damned McLeod."

A branch flew in his direction and he ducked just in time to avoid it. Tristan's eyes widened at noting Merida was bent at the waist, seeking another weapon.

"I do not wish to marry a damned Ross either." She threw the thick stick with force. The guard dodged the second projectile, but it bounced off his shoulder and bounced on Tristan's head.

"Stop at once," Tristan called out and stood up straight.

A rock flew in his direction and barely missed him. He and the guard hurried to find cover behind a short wall.

Tristan lifted to look over the wall. "Merida…" He stopped short when something hit him square in the forehead.

"I would not marry ye ever," she called out and a cascade of pebbles fell over him and the guard.

A second guard approached and when a rock hit him, he ducked behind the wall next to Tristan. "I believe to have just seen Ethan McLeod," he said, frowning in Merida's direction. "What did ye do?"

A larger rock zinged by. It bounced off the wall, hitting Tristan's shoulder. He flinched and let out a sigh. "Go get our horses. Tell Ruari, but no one else."

The two men ran off and he straightened. Ignoring the next two items thrown at him, he charged toward Merida.

At seeing him run toward her, she spun and dashed away. Tristan chased her, not really trying to catch her until the fiery lass raced into the keep. Then he hurried back to where the guards waited with their horses.

"Where are ye headed?" the head guard asked at the gates. Although they were not closed and the guard didn't have any right to question him, Tristan decided it was best to keep the peace.

"To meet my brother's messenger."

The guard nodded, seeming satisfied with the explanation. It mattered not if he believed it or not, but he needed a reply in case the laird or someone in the family asked.

"Which direction did he go?" Tristan asked the guard who'd brought the message about Ethan. The man silently motioned to the west. Not the direction Tristan expected.

Twice, Tristan had to stop and throw up. Once again, his stomach lurched but he ignored it. Already, they'd lost valuable time and, at this point, he doubted they'd catch up to Ethan.

"He must have doubled back to go east and we missed it." Ruari, who'd ridden ahead, returned to where Tristan was. "Tis futile to continue unless we split up and go in all four directions."

Tristan scanned the area. There was a large loch surrounded by woods. A small village nestled next to the western shores. "We can ask at the village to see if anyone has seen him. If not, I agree, we lost him."

Too angry at himself for drinking too much, he clenched his jaw when once again his stomach tightened with the telltale sign. "Go on ahead, I have to dismount for a moment."

Ruari gave him an understanding look. "Take yer time, Tristan. There is little for us to do now."

The coolness of the breeze helped him regain some semblance of well-being on the ride back. Tristan continued to scan for any signs of Ethan. He couldn't help but wonder what would have happened if they'd caught up with the bastard. No doubt, the wedding would have been called off.

Chapter Eleven

PAIGE SEARCHED OUT her husband's sister, still confused at what to think of the happenings of the night before. How she'd keep the secret from Alec, she wasn't sure. He would know something was wrong whenever Ethan came around her. Alec had become so attuned to her feelings that he often remarked on how she felt even before she admitted it.

"Merida?" She walked into the empty chamber, surprised not to find her. Merida never went down for first meal without coming for her.

Rushing to the window, she looked out to see Merida standing atop a short wall in the garden. Her friend held a hand up to her eyes as she looked out. In the distance, four horsemen approached and Merida scrambled from the wall, but remained in the garden.

"How peculiar," Paige said in a low voice as she hurried out of the room, down the corridor and then down the stairway.

Still in the garden, Merida continued to gaze out to where the men rode closer. She turned to Paige. "I was about to come get ye. I am famished."

"What were ye doing standing atop the wall? Ye could have fallen." Paige's chastisement went unanswered as Merida kept an eye out.

"Merida?" Paige said, touching her arm. "Is something amiss?"

"I am not getting married," Merida replied, glaring at the approaching men. "I do not think they caught Ethan."

At the name, Paige turned to look at the riders. They were Tristan Ross, his cousin and two others.

"How do ye know?"

"Because they are glowering," Merida replied. "Come, hurry, let us go inside before they come closer."

Paige had to almost run to keep up with Merida, who yanked her forward. "Why are ye not getting married?"

"Because he insulted me," Merida said. "Besides, he does not wish to marry me. He said so this very morning."

Paige's eyes widened and she stopped in her tracks. "What did ye say? What did he say?"

"Goodness, Paige, I cannot speak of this on an empty stomach. I do not wish to be near that man. Let us go to the kitchens."

"Yer brother returned home?" Paige asked, her chest tightening. What would happen if Ethan changed the story and told Alec she was the one to make advances? "What do ye think he will tell Alec?"

"He will only be there for a day or so and then off to check the borders and such. Da sent two men to ensure he does. Besides, Alec will not believe anything Ethan says."

Not as sure, Paige followed Merida to the kitchens. Instantly, the aroma of stew and baking bread sent all worries away. The cook, who wasn't as kind as Rose, the McLeod cook, but just as efficient, greeted them by motioning to a side table for them to sit at. "Stay out of the way. We have much to do," she admonished while slapping a wooden platter with meat, cheese and mutton in front of them. Next, a girl put a chunk of crusty bread on the same tray and returned to her duties.

Merida seemed to have forgotten all her troubles as well, smiling as she bit into butter-slathered bread.

"Are ye not worried about what yer father will say if ye refuse to marry?" Paige whispered. "Ye simply cannot refuse."

With a long sigh, Merida nodded. "I am considering what to do. I threw rocks and sticks at him, ye know?" An impish grin lit her already pretty face. "After my behavior, which I admit was one of a ten-year-old girl, Tristan may not wish to marry me." She took a second bite of bread and scowled. "He should be the one to call it off."

"I doubt either of ye have much choice," Paige said, considering how she could help her friend get out of the situation. In part, however, Paige felt that there was a type of bond between Merida and Tristan. They suited one another and although both had strong personalities, Tristan seemed to be a lot more patient than Merida. His manner complemented Merida's more headstrong ways.

"No matter," Merida said. "I will speak to Da and insist he ask the Mackenzie to reconsider."

They ate in silence for a few minutes more and, finally, Paige had her fill. She placed a hand on Merida's lower arm. "Ye have to accept things, Merida. Tis best for ye not to seek any changes. It will look bad upon our clan and yer father."

Merida frowned for a long moment, her expression turning solemn. "He does not wish to marry me."

"Tis the fact the marriage is forced. Besides, he and ye are from warring clans."

Paige realized Merida's feelings were hurt and she understood it. Somehow, she would find a way to speak to Tristan. The man needed to make amends before the marriage took place.

BY THE TIME Tristan released his horse and washed up, it was too late to eat. His stomach grumbled, empty now after getting sick so many times. At least his headache had finally abated and he felt considerably better.

From where he stood, just outside the stables, he watched steam coming from the kitchen chimney. His mouth watered as he considered going and asking for a light repast to hold him until dinner.

Without him actually willing it, his legs began the walk toward the kitchen door. At the entryway, he peered inside to see Merida seated with Alec's wife. The women were deep in discussion so they did not see him. If he walked in then, Merida had access to many items she could throw at him. Best to wait.

"Tristan Ross." He turned to find one of the Mackenzie's guards. "A Ross party approaches."

He followed the guard to the gates just as his guardsmen returned along with his uncle, Gregor, and two more. His uncle nodded in acknowledgement, his gaze instantly moving to where the McLeod guards kept watch.

"Tis not comforting to see that." Gregor motioned toward the McLeods with his head. He dismounted and allowed the guards to take his steed.

"Uncle, I am glad ye are here. I need counsel as to what to do. Perhaps ye can speak with the Mackenzie. Find a solution to this forced marriage between our clans. It will never work."

It was only moments later that they were seated in the Mackenzie's study, along with Laird McLeod.

***

"MY LAIRD WISHES to impart that he cedes to yer ruling in this matter, however, he also asked that I remind ye of our ongoing feud. Although a truce may come from our joining with the McLeods with this marriage, it does not mean those that seek revenge or retribution for what was lost will adhere to it." As always, his uncle knew how to phrase things in a way that seemed to leave everything under another's control. Self-important men like the Mackenzie rarely could tell they were being manipulated.

Tristan listened and studied how his uncle spoke, his mannerisms and tones. It was interesting how both the McLeod and the Mackenzie both listened without interrupting. His uncle had always accompanied his father when meeting with lairds. Now he wished that he'd come along from the beginning. Perhaps they'd not be tied up in a marriage with their enemy.

"Another thing I would like to add," his uncle continued, "is that we have a truce in place, which we expect to remain in force with or without the marriage. My laird wishes for ye to understand that continuing the battling is not what we wish for our clan."

The Mackenzie nodded. "What of revenge? It would start another clan war. Does yer laird not wish it?"

"Whether I marry Merida McLeod or not, our wish to avenge our father will not wane." Tristan had to speak up. His uncle slid him a glance, but didn't seemed perturbed by his outburst.

"Of course, my nephews will never welcome yer second son." Gregor spoke to the McLeod this time. "And I cannot ever guarantee there will not be some sort of retribution for what he did."

"The marriage means our clans will be joined. The agreement must be that ye will not seek to harm any member of my family." The McLeod's voice was even. Obviously, the man was also well-versed in negotiations. "I agree that his actions were rash and without provocation, but he is my son and I do not wish him dead."

"He killed my father," Tristan said.

"And what of all the fathers that ye have killed since?" the McLeod rebutted.

"Tis not the same thing and ye know it."

"Is that what ye tell the orphans? The widows?"

"Enough," the Mackenzie spoke in a soft tone. "I find it interesting that yer laird did not come here and sent ye in his stead. Inform him that he must come, and soon."

"As the new laird, with spring just now beginning, there is much to do. As the McLeod can state, caring for many after a war weighs heavy. He feels his duty is to the people right now."

"I must leave soon," the McLeod said. "Tis too many days to be gone. Although my eldest is a good leader, I feel the obligation to be with my clan."

"After the wedding tomorrow, I understand ye will wish to take yer leave." The Mackenzie met Tristan's gaze. "Ye gave yer word, therefore, it will happen." He then turned his attention to the McLeod. "Ye have lost more than they. I find yer willingness to negotiate admirable."

The McLeod looked to Gregor and then to Tristan. "I was friends with yer brother…and father and held him in high regard. That he was killed so senselessly grieves me greatly. If it could be undone, I would be the first to see to it. On behalf of Clan McLeod, I offer my apologies."

There was silence and Tristan's throat constricted. He'd known that the McLeod and his father were friendly, but hearing the hoarseness in his tone made it obvious he would have never agreed to what his son did.

"Ye do not owe us an apology," Tristan said. "But thank ye."

"When the sun is highest tomorrow, there will be a marriage ceremony," the Mackenzie said with a gleeful smile. "Cook is preparing an astonishing feast."

Tristan fought not to roll his eyes. Instead, he nodded at the annoying man and accepted the cup of whisky placed in front of him.

"A toast to peace between Clan Ross and Clan McLeod," the Mackenzie said, raising his cup. Tristan, his uncle and Clyde McLeod lifted their cups as well. Just before taking a drink, Tristan noted the McLeod's gaze traveling over him.

The man was deciding if he was worthy of his beautiful daughter. If Tristan was to be honest, he was not. Not only did he not care for her family, but also he wasn't sure he'd make a good husband to Merida McLeod. Tristan placed his still full cup down, hoping the Mackenzie didn't notice. Just the smell of whisky made his empty stomach lurch.

They walked out of the keep moments later and Tristan took a deep breath of air.

"Thank ye for trying," he said to his uncle. "I was sure even ye would not change the man's mind."

His uncle watched a flock of geese fly overhead. "How do ye get along with the lass?"

"She is quite headstrong. Just this morning, she attacked me and two guards with sticks and stones."

His uncle frowned. "What did ye do?"

"Nothing," Tristan lied.

Chapter Twelve

The morning was sunny and although the air was crisp, Merida wasn't cold. Guiding her horse out through the gates of the keep, she allowed Duin to meander to wherever it wished. Her mind wasn't in the moment, but on the events that would happen later that day.

Even after telling her father of what she'd overheard Tristan say, he was unbendable in that the marriage would take place. In truth, she didn't protest much. There were lines of exhaustion around his eyes and although he didn't raise his voice, it was evident he'd lose patience quickly.

"The marriage is tomorrow. I suggest ye go and prepare. Do not do anything to embarrass me." He'd dismissed her promptly.

Merida had nodded. "I will be ready come the appointed time."

At the evening meal the night before, Tristan had been present, seeming unfazed and even laughing with his cousin and uncle. Apparently, the upcoming wedding was not as worrisome to him. Of course not, he'd return to his home and all that was familiar. Merida couldn't help but glare at him when he looked in her direction.

When her mother elbowed her none-to-gently in the ribs, she let out a sigh and forced a smile.

Birdsong brought Merida back to the present and upon seeing

several birds on a branch singing, she relaxed.

"Ye are too far from the keep," Tristan said, coming up from behind her. "Ye should take a guard or two when out and about."

As if sensing her tension, the birds stopped singing and flew away. Merida looked over her shoulder, noting not only that Tristan watched her with curiosity, but that the keep was out of sight.

"I came here to get some peace," she snapped. "Why are ye here?"

"I followed ye," he replied with aggravating nonchalance. "We need to speak about yesterday."

Merida pulled Duin around to face Tristan. "What about yesterday? That ye insulted me or that ye went after my brother?"

"Both," he replied. "What I said was not meant for yer ears."

"Ye do not want to marry me, that is one thing, but to insult my clan is not something I will allow."

His eyes went flat. "Do ye expect me to respect the clan of the man who murdered my father?"

"The clan has nothing to do with what my brother did."

With an unreadable expression, he studied her, his hazel gaze unwavering. "Ye must know that because we marry does not mean my clan will not continue to seek retribution."

"Ye plan to continue to be at war with us?"

"Nay, but yer brother will pay for what he did."

It was hard to keep the tears of frustration at bay. Merida blinked at the thought that her brother could eventually die by her husband's hand.

"Guards are coming," he said, interrupting her thoughts. "They look to be McLeods." His voice took a lower, growl-like tone. "We should return."

They rode side-by-side toward the keep. Upon meeting with the guards, Merida instructed them to return as well. The men insisted on following them, which she could tell did not please Tristan. However, he didn't say anything.

Just as they reached the gates, Tristan turned to her. "I do look forward to marrying ye. Tis not ye that makes me hesitate, know that."

Merida could only nod as the guards dismounted and neared. She waved them away. "I am taking Duin to the corral myself."

Tristan dismounted and she did as well, guiding her horse toward the stables and corrals. "I would like to take my horse with me," she said and lifted her gaze to him. "And, I will go visit my parents regularly."

"Anything else?" Tristan asked, not looking at her, but straight ahead.

"I wish to have freedom to ride Duin outside the keep walls."

"With guards, yes."

For now, she let it pass as she wracked her brain to ensure he heard all her demands before they married. "I would like Mother and Paige to visit. Also, my companion, Elsa, will come with me."

"I do not have a problem with any of it. I will ensure my brother agrees to it. We do not hold Alec or Paige to blame for what happened. However, we have to give the people time to become accustomed to our marriage before having McLeods traveling freely through our lands."

"Of course, I understand."

They reached the corrals and Merida went about ensuring Duin had food and water before making her way back to the house.

Tristan walked away after his horse was taken by a stable lad, seeming to understand she needed time alone.

Soon, she'd be bathed, dressed and prepared for the wedding ceremony. As she crossed the threshold, her stomach tumbled at the realization that on this day, her life would change forever.

PEOPLE FROM THE surrounding villages soon filled the great room, overflowing out to the courtyard. Pipers played lively tunes and children ran circles around people, darting here and there in their games.

A tent was erected, under which ladies sat on blankets, gossiping happily in cheerful circles.

There were camps set up outside the gates with chopped wood already collected for bonfires that would keep everyone warm when evening came.

Lady Mackenzie, Lady McLeod, Paige and the Mackenzie's cook rushed to and fro calling out orders to servants, ensuring everything was just so.

Merida stood at the top of the stairs for a long moment, watching the commotion with interest. It seemed the women below were having the time of their lives as they glided here and there, pointing to items that needed rearranging or discussing the evening's meal offerings.

No one seemed to remember her at the moment and it suited her just fine. She'd bathed and several servants had come to assist braiding her hair and wrapping it about her head in a beautiful, intricate style.

In truth, the entire affair was to be grand, almost as if she were, indeed, marrying a Mackenzie. The great room was twice the size of the one at her home. Not only were many coming from Mackenzie lands but, overnight, McLeods piled into wagons had arrived.

Whether out of alliance or curiosity, Merida wasn't sure why her clan's people had traveled so far. If she were to guess, it was because they wanted to see with their own eyes that the McLeod's daughter was, indeed, marrying a Ross.

Moments later, her mother appeared at the top of the stairs. Cheeks flushed and eyes sparkling, she tugged Merida by the hand to the bedchamber. "Isn't it grand? I never hoped to have a wedding so well attended and with so much..." she waved her hand in the air, unsure of what word to use.

"Everyone is just overly excited at winter finally ending and warmer weather," Merida replied. "They are celebrating the warmth of the season more than my wedding."

Her mother smiled widely. "And the food. Oh, Merida, wait until ye see the grand feast Lady Mackenzie is having prepared. They've slaughtered three large hogs."

Merida's stomach tightened. Her palms became moist and her heart thudded erratically. "I hope the hogs take everyone's attention. I haven't a proper dress for such an occasion."

"Come," her mother said, guiding her upstairs to a chamber that had been set aside for the wedding preparations.

With a secretive smile, her mother went to a wardrobe against the back wall and pulled the right door open. A beautiful cream gown hung on the door, the bottom of the dress spilling in a puddle of softness on the floor. Unable to help it, Merida gasped and hurried to it, her mouth agape.

"Where did it come from?"

"One of Lady Mackenzie's nieces had it made for her wedding, but later decided on a different one. It was being held for one of the younger daughters, but the girls insist they would rather choose their own." Her mother spread the skirt out. "Lady Mackenzie was generous enough to gift it to ye."

Merida neared and lifted the skirts to get a better look. Although woven, somehow the dressmaker had managed to create the lightest fabric she'd ever seen. It was soft to the touch and yet sturdy and would keep the chill away.

"It's beautiful," Merida said, running a finger across the lacings down the center of the blouse. There was a light sage-colored edging that made the dress both elegant and with a hint of the Highlands.

There was a discreet knock and Paige entered. Her lips curved. "Do ye like it?"

Elsa walked in behind Paige with a tray of food and her mouth fell open. "Wondrous," she whispered, her eyes locked on the gown.

Merida could only nod. Once again, she was nervous and worried about what the day would bring.

Once she was dressed, servants came in and set about exchanging the linens on the bed. A screen was set up just as one came into the room. It would have blocked a view of the bed from the corridor, however the fabric was sheer. Several chairs were brought and placed on the opposite side of the screen from the bed.

Merida walked around the screen and peered through the sheer fabric. She could see through it, not clearly, but certainly enough to know whoever sat there would see more than she felt comfortable with.

"Why is this necessary?" she asked, stalking around it to where her mother and Paige both met her question with uncertainty. "I am not marrying a laird's son, but a second born. There is no need for this depravity."

Her mother neared the screen and shook her head. "I do not like this garish display for others. Lady Mackenzie attends royal court often. It must be how it's done there."

Paige was flummoxed. She looked from Lady McLeod to Merida. "What exactly is going to happen? Why the screen and chairs?"

"The bedding ceremony," Merida's mother replied. "I suppose it must be witnessed since our clans are at war and ye are a laird's first-born daughter."

"Witnessed?" Paige's wide eyes met Merida's. "Have ye no choice in this?"

Merida snorted in the most unladylike fashion. "Oh, I believe I do. I will not do it."

"It's the most unpleasant thing I have ever heard of," Paige said, going to the other side of the screen and poking at it. "Most unpleasant," she repeated.

Not wanting to dwell on it for the moment, Merida went to peer out the window. The courtyard was now fuller than earlier. People spilled out from the great room where the ceremony would take place. Merida would have preferred the chapel, but the one in the keep was surprisingly small.

"Tis best to get this over with," she mumbled. "Is everyone ready now?"

A hush fell over the great room when Merida descended the stairs. Soft murmurs were swiftly hushed as she passed people to where her father stood.

Merida kept her gaze forward, but not really seeing anything. Her father took her arm and escorted her to the front of the room. Once there, she finally noticed that Tristan stood, with his uncle beside him. Wearing his plaid tartan of deep green and blue, he stood proudly, the Ross broach on the left side of his broad chest.

By the dampness of his hair, he'd bathed recently and smelled of outdoors and fresh pine.

Their gazes clashed and she could only see certainty in his hazel gaze. Both turned to the minister when he cleared his throat to announce that they'd begin the ceremony.

Merida kept her voice even when saying her vows, her eyes never moving from Tristan's. He radiated certainty and it gave her strength not to collapse since her knees shook uncontrollably.

"Yer vows," the minister said.

"I, Tristan Roderick Ross, swear to take ye to be my wife and my spouse and I pledge to ye the faith of my body, that I will be faithful to ye and loyal with my body and my goods and that I will keep ye in sickness and in health and in whatever condition it will please the Lord to place ye, and that I shall not exchange ye for better or worse until the end." He recited the vows easily with a clear and concise voice that left no room for criticism that he was not in agreement to marry her.

For it, she was glad. Somehow, the clarity of his commitment gave her strength to say her own vows.

When they were finally pronounced husband and wife, the priest asked that they seal their union with a kiss. Once again, it was as if the air left the room as everyone waited to see what would happen.

Merida turned to Tristan and lifted her face. When his lips covered hers, she closed her eyes, allowing everyone and everything to disappear for that instant. If nothing else, she wanted to memorize the moment she became a wife and sworn to a man for the rest of her life.

Surprisingly, the kiss lingered. When he cupped her jaw and deepened the kiss, there was murmuring. When he lifted up, she opened her eyes and he winked at her. She couldn't help but smile. The man was much too self-assured in her opinion.

***

MUCH TOO SOON after the celebration began, Merida's mother and Lady Mackenzie came to whisk her away. Merida did her best to protest, claiming not to have eaten yet. But unfortunately, everyone had witnessed her devouring a plate of food.

Every step she took up the stairs seemed to cause more and more attention. Merida made the mistake of looking back, only to meet a sea of eyes watching her. Would this night ever end? Hopefully, she could close her eyes and block what happened until the next morning.

"What a beautiful chemise," Lady Mackenzie said, holding up the article of clothing that had been unpacked from her trunks.

Merida looked to her mother. "Why is that here?"

"I packed a few extra things, just in case." Her mother gave her a sheepish smile. "One never knows."

She wanted to glare at her mother, but decided it was best not to in front of Lady Mackenzie and several other curious women who'd come into the room under the guise of helping.

"I do not require more than Mother, Elsa and Paige's help to undress and put on the chemise," Merida informed the group. "Honestly, this is all a bit daunting and embarrassing." She looked to Lady Mackenzie. "I do not plan to be taken in front of witnesses. Ye should inform everyone."

Lady Mackenzie ignored her and motioned a young woman over. "Help take down her hair and ye," she pointed at another, "turn down the bedding."

Her dress was removed and she stood bare in front of everyone. Modesty was not a priority it seemed. And Merida considered, being that they thought she was about to be taken in front of everyone that could squeeze in behind the flimsy screen, she shouldn't be so concerned.

The chemise was lifted over her head, the fabric falling down her chilled body, doing little to warm her since the fabric was much too thin to be practical. Two women unbraided her hair and brushed it down. Then she was helped into the bed.

It turned out Merida did need the help because as soon as she was sitting on the pillows, noise in the corridor announced the arrival of the bridegroom and others.

There was commotion as people found their places. To Merida's astonishment, not only did Lady Mackenzie remain in the room, but also the priest and two other men she didn't know. She met her mother's gaze, but then looked away when her mother smiled.

Why was everyone so happy? She was about to be humiliated.

Tristan entered. As usual, his expression was unreadable. He didn't seem at all discomfited by the current situation. At the side of the bed, he removed his tartan and allowed it to fall to the floor. The silence in the room was deafening.

Merida decided the best thing to do was to keep her gaze on Tristan and when she did, she found strength. He slid into the bed and immediately came over her. Then to her shock, he took her mouth, his lips pressing against hers with passion.

Unable to keep from it, she wrapped her arms about his neck and shoulders, holding him and using him as a barrier from the witnesses.

As Tristan continued to kiss her, he pushed her chemise up and settled between her legs.

"No," Merida said firmly. "I will not do this in front of people."

"Ignore them. Close yer eyes," Tristan murmured while pressing his lips to just beneath her ear.

"I said no." Merida pushed him back. "Tell them to leave or I will scream."

There was a twinkle in Tristan's gaze and he lifted up. He then turned to the people in the room. "Leave us. We will provide proof of consummation."

"It must be witnessed," the minister said.

Tristan turned to look at the man. "If ye do not leave, I will throw ye out the window myself, old man."

After one last glare at them, the priest hurried out.

There were rumblings but, one by one, everyone else soon followed.

At the soft closing of the door, Merida let out a breath. "Now ye may proceed."

Tristan chuckled. "Ye are admirable, Wife."

Wife.

The sensations of his hands traveling down her body, the pressure of his lips over hers took over and, soon, Merida was kissing him back. Every inch of her skin cried out for his touch and she dug her fingers into the fabric of his tunic.

He somehow managed to spread her legs wider apart. How, exactly, Merida was not aware. When he rubbed his sex against hers, she squirmed at the reaction her body had. Tendrils of heat pooled in her core and down her legs.

"Wrap yer legs about my waist," Tristan instructed and she did as he said.

There were soft murmurs outside the door. It sounded as if some people were becoming unsettled. Not caring what they felt, Merida wanted to laugh at someone else experiencing discomfort.

Tristan slid one hand between them and took himself in hand. Curious to know how he felt, she did the same and he allowed it. Touching her way down his front, she then wrapped her hand around his sex. His member was hard and thick, making her wonder how it would be that he could enter her and fit.

Once again, he took her mouth, pushed her hand away and guided his shaft to her entrance. "Relax," he said between kisses.

When he drove into her, Merida cried out in shock. The pain was sharp, but momentary. Soon, her mind went to how fully he filled her, the strange sensation of being stretched and joined with him, not quite unbearable.

"Take yer time, relax," Tristan said, keeping still.

Then as she began to relax, he began to move. He pulled out and then thrust back in several times until she wanted him to do so faster.

Outside in the corridor, there was a clearing of throats, but it didn't stop Tristan from continuing. Merida, however, wondered if people had their ears to the door, or perhaps peered through the keyhole.

"Look at me." Tristan turned her head to face him. "Tis only us here that matters."

It was only moments later that he stiffened and spilled. Merida wasn't sure what to do. She'd been enjoying the moment until recalling the witnesses and, after that, she could not relax.

"Ye may enter," Tristan called out, sitting up. Merida scrambled up to the pillows and wrapped her arms around her knees. "Idiots," she mumbled.

Her mother and Lady Mackenzie entered to inspect the sheets, but didn't near the bed. The women spoke for a moment and then pronounced the marriage was consummated without actually looking.

"I am not sure how I feel in this moment," Merida said to Tristan who lay beside her. "What happens now?"

He turned to face her. "We spend more time here together in the chamber. We are not expected at first meal."

A shiver went down her body at considering that she'd share her bed with him all night. Merida tapped his shoulder. "Did ye enjoy it?"

"Not so much."

"Me either."

His lips curved. "I will ensure ye do next time."

Surely, there wasn't anything different to be done. Although she enjoyed his kisses and caresses, the actual joining was not what she'd expected. It was overwhelming and a bit uncomfortable. It wasn't exactly something she would like to do again.

"Ye think too much," Tristan said, rolling to face her. "There is more to joining than what we did earlier."

Unsure if he said it to ensure she allowed it again, Merida frowned. "What else could there possibly be?"

"I will show ye," Tristan replied and tugged at her chemise. "First, this must be done away with."

Once the chemise was off, he then tugged his own tunic over his head. They lay next to each other, bare as the day they were born. She ran her hands down his chest, remembering the wounds that almost killed him. "They remain quite red," she murmured.

The candlelight was enough that she could see that although very visible, his wounds had healed. "Ye had a good healer," she murmured, noting the lack of darkening around the wounds.

"I had two very good healers," he replied, pulling her hand to his lips. "Did I ever thank ye for saving my life?"

"Yes, by living." Merida smiled.

"Ye must take me to meet the man who returned me to my family so that I can thank him properly as well."

Merida nodded. "Aye, I can. He lives on McLeod lands however."

Instead of speaking more, he traced the pads of his fingers up from her waist, hesitating at her left breast. Then, ever so slowly, circled the tip, sending awareness from where he touched throughout her body.

Once the pink tip of her breast grew rigid, Tristan leaned over and took it into his mouth. His tongue followed the same pattern his finger had, but the sensations were stronger and Merida gasped in air while threading her hand through his hair.

Need slammed into her and she arched up to his touch. Inexperienced in how to react, all Merida hoped was that he would know how to quench the fire.

She stiffened at his hand traveling up her thigh, unsure if she was prepared for another intrusion. But when his slid a finger through her folds and found the center, she cried out at the wonderful stirs that assaulted.

There wasn't a way to explain what happened. All Merida knew was that never in her life had she experienced so much at the same time. Tristan circled the nub in the center of her sex until she began calling out his name.

"More. Oh, Tristan." Merida was losing control but, at the same time, it was terrifying.

When he mounted her and teased at her entrance, Merida lifted, needing to be filled, wanting more than anything the beautiful ending that teased at the edges of recognition.

Ever so slowly, he pushed in, taking time to ensure she adjusted. All the while, his mouth teased at hers, his hands holding her breasts, both thumbs circling her nipples.

"Yes," Merida said over and over. She knew it would be different this time. Already she was overfilled with pleasure.

Finally fully inside, Tristan let out a long moan and began moving, his hips lifting and lowering in a steady rhythm. He pulled out almost completely before thrusting in until fully inside as Merida urged him to continue, to move faster and take her to full completion.

Her cries intermingled with his grunts of pleasure as they continued, each urging the other over the cliff to what awaited.

Although terrified when everything began spinning, Merida could not control herself any longer. With a loud cry, she let go, floating high before crashing down. Every single part of her body was rigid in anticipation until, finally, the last waves of her climax ebbed.

Tristan's movements were hard and fast, his race to finish seeming to elude him. Merida grasped his shoulders to keep from being slammed against the headboard, but on he continued, his muscular body becoming drenched in sweat.

He was a majestic sight, skin gleaming, his face tight and muscles bunching with each movement. Stirrings like before surged, but this time not as strong as he lifted her bottom and held her in place so that he could enter deeper.

When he finally stiffened, sending currents of pleasure through Merida, his hot seed spilled over onto the bed.

He collapsed atop her, panting, and Merida ran her hands down his back, her sex tightening around his as she finally settled from the lovemaking.

"How wonderful," Merida said, barely able to keep her eyes open.

"Mmmm," Tristan replied, rolling off of her and pulling her against his side.

Moments later, soft snores filled the chamber as a maid tiptoed in to douse the candles.

Both slept until late the next morning, not having to find an excuse for missing the morning meal. Sometime during the night, Merida had wakened and explored Tristan's body.

She'd mimicked his movement, sliding her hands up his torso, teasing the tips of his chest until he'd begun to breathe harder. Emboldened by his reactions, she'd then dared to touch between his legs. The sack and dormant staff were so different than anything she'd ever known. At her curious touch, he'd become aroused.

How interesting that at noticing his reaction, her body immediately responded. The lovemaking had begun with him sliding into her, moving lazily and without hurry. It was so different that Merida understood there were many ways, depending on the mood, to make love.

Passion took over and, soon, his movements became faster until both climaxed together.

His hands traveling over her body woke her to find that the sun was up.

Surely he didn't mean to make love again. Merida pushed his hand away. "We cannot. Tis light."

Tristan's soft chuckle made her giggle. "Why do ye laugh?"

"People can make love whenever they wish, not only during the night hours, Wife."

"Oh," Merida replied, but did not utter another word because his mouth took hers.

CHAPTER THIRTEEN

HIS UNCLE WAS given a chamber inside the main house and Tristan found him looking out the window, seeming deep in thought. He didn't turn upon Tristan entering.

"We should leave immediately," Tristan said. "I do not wish to remain here any longer. The Mackenzie has gotten his way. There is naught else for us to remain."

His uncle turned. "Did ye not enjoy yer wedding night?"

"That is not what is important." Tristan did his best to not dwell on the fact that he had quite enjoyed his time with Merida.

"I agree we should leave, but scouts should be sent ahead to ensure the travel will be safe. Ye will travel with a wife, Tristan, and not to mention, a lass from another clan."

He wasn't convinced of any dangers. Not only had his messenger gone back, but his uncle and several guards had returned without any problems. "Nay, we leave within the hour. We can travel until dark and continue on in the morning."

"Very well. I will inform the guardsmen to prepare to leave."

In truth, he would have preferred to travel ahead and reach his keep before the party that would include his McLeod wife and whoever she brought along. Not to mention the many stops they'd have to make since women were not accustomed to riding nonstop to a distant destination.

In his opinion, it would have been best that way since it would allow for him to prepare his clan for the presence of a McLeod among them. Even without preparation, it would be a difficult transition not just for his clan, but also for Merida.

His uncle left to go see about the guards and Tristan went on to the great room to find Merida's father and inform him they were to leave.

As soon as he sat at the table where the McLeod and his wife were, a servant brought him drink and food. He nodded his appreciation, but his mind was already preoccupied with the ride ahead. Nonetheless, it would be a long ride and knowing it was best to eat, he pulled the plate closer.

"We must leave immediately. Within the hour." His announcement was met with shocked looks.

"So soon?" Lady McLeod got to her feet. "Can ye not wait a day at least."

"Nay," Tristan replied. "We have lingered overly long already. There is much to do back at my homelands. Spring arrives and I have duties to see to."

The McLeod stood and looked to the doorway. "Ye do not give me time to send for my guardsmen, a scout to ensure safe travels for my daughter. I cannot afford to give up any of my escorts right now."

"It will be well. I have enough guards to keep yer daughter safe."

As his wife hurried away, the McLeod gave him an annoyed look. "I hope that in the future, ye take yer wife more into consideration."

"Tis what has to be done, whether a long or short farewell, ye were aware that Merida would leave with me. I will ensure for her safety. Ye and yer wife are welcome to come visit." He hesitated. "Or I will bring her to ye. It may be safer that way."

"That will take some time. Ye are well aware of it. Neither of our clans has been fully informed of what transpired here."

Tristan clenched his jaw and let out a breath through his nostrils. Never did he think to have to explain his decisions to a McLeod. And yet, the McLeod was in his rights as a father to make demands over his daughter.

The man's eyes narrowed and he lowered his voice. "Know this, if any harm befalls my daughter, I will not care if I die, but I will find ye."

He stormed away.

Too annoyed at being chastised, Tristan barely tasted the food. He stood and went to find the Mackenzie.

Once he was allowed into the Mackenzie's study, Tristan gave him the same news as earlier. Unlike the McLeods, the Mackenzie was understanding of his need to return to his keep. "See that yer brother comes to visit later this season."

"Aye, I will," Tristan replied and waited a beat. "Know that although we are allies with ye, we do not feel beholden to ye. Our lands remain ours, as do yers. However, if ever the need comes for ye to need anything, we will respond."

Unexpectedly, the Mackenzie chuckled. "Ye make a good leader. Yer brother is fortunate to have ye to speak on his behalf. Likewise, Clan Mackenzie will be available to ye."

Tristan wanted to ask if the same offer was made to the McLeods but knew the Mackenzie would rebuff the question. Instead, he nodded and left.

Already, his mind was ahead, planning the best route to return quickly but also ensure for easy travel with a cart and wagon.

MERIDA HAD JUST finished dressing when her mother and Paige burst into the room. Upon seeing her mother was crying, her chest tightened. "What has happened? Is Da…"

"'Tis not that," Paige interrupted. "Ye're leaving."

"I know," Merida said, consoling her mother. "Let us spend the day together. I wish to talk and perhaps go for a walk to the loch."

Her mother shook her head. "'Tis not possible. Yer husband is preparing the mounts. He means for ye to leave immediately."

"What?" Merida rushed to the window, threw the covering aside and leaned out. Sure enough, in the center of the courtyard were her husband, his uncle and a contingent of Ross guardsmen. They looked to be packing up the horses, tying bundles to their saddles and walking back and forth to a wagon.

"He did not say anything to me about this." Merida's heart threatened to beat out of her chest. "Why did he not speak to me?"

Her mother neared and pulled her into an embrace. "At this point, it matters not. We must help ye prepare." She turned to Paige. "Fetch Elsa and Hilda and two lads to come help us pack and send another to fetch food for Merida to break her fast and also ask that a food basket be prepared for her to take."

Too shocked to speak, she could only stand in the center of the room and blink back tears. This was not how she expected the day would go. Not only did Tristan not say a word to her, but also for him to go forth with such an important decision without allowing her opinion resonated of how much her life was to change.

It took a lot of fortitude not to race out the door and confront Tristan. Instead, she went to the nearest trunk and searched for a traveling outfit.

Time seemed to speed through. Between Elsa and Lady Mackenzie's maids, all the packing was completed promptly, her hair plaited and put up in a sensible style and she was ready to go.

Head held high, she walked to the doorway. Her companion, Elsa, sniffed and she turned. "Do not cry. Ye had a choice to remain behind. I did not."

Elsa's eyes widened. "Aye, I am sorry. I will try not to cry." She wasn't successful as a tear trickled down her reddened cheek.

Merida let out a sigh. "Try not to cry when we get outside then." Ensuring to avoid looking at either her mother or Paige, she marched out, down the stairwell and through the front door.

Unlike her current mood, the day was perfect. Warm with just a few fluffy clouds hovering in the bright blue sky, spring was apparent. A light breeze blew that would make traveling easy, bringing a respite to both traveler and horses from the bright sun.

Ensuring to keep her gaze flat, she did not look to Tristan, but to the lads who carried her trunks. "See that they are on one side of the wagon. My companion needs a comfortable place to sit. Place folded blankets there." She pointed and then turned to another set of young men who brought Elsa's smaller trunk and a basket.

"The small trunk can be put next to mine. The basket should be placed up toward the front so that Elsa is able to reach into it."

Her mother neared to inspect how things were set up. "Ensure there are another set of blankets for ye to lay upon to rest." She nodded, satisfied when a maid hurried up with a neatly folded set of bedding.

Out of the corners of her eyes, she caught sight of Tristan pacing back and forth. She refused to allow him to make her hurry. If anything, she'd make doubly sure everything was just right before announcing she was ready to travel.

"Where is Duin?" she asked, looking for her horse.

The Ross guards exchanged looks. "He will not allow anyone near him."

Her lips twitched at Duin's defiance, matching her own. "I will go see about him."

"Nay, we do not have time," Tristan said as he approached her. "He can remain behind."

When she turned to him, he must have seen something in her expression because his eyebrows rose just a bit.

"Duin does not allow my own clansmen near him either. He comes with me." She spoke each word clearly, not leaving any room for misinterpretation.

The muscles at his jawline moved. He was having a hard time keeping his temper in check. Good. So was she.

"Very well. But do not take too long. We must leave and travel as far as possible before sundown."

With a guard and Paige alongside her, Merida made her way to the corrals. "Tis ridiculous to leave so late in the day. If we left at dawn, we could possibly arrive the same day. But nay, the man wants to do things his way and put everyone at risk to show his power..."

The guard cleared his throat, making her wonder if he was hiding a chuckle. Paige gasped. "Merida, do not be so bold. Ye have to obey yer husband."

"I am allowed an opinion, am I not?" she snapped, but then softened. "Paige, ye are fortunate to have married someone ye chose. My brother gives ye heed to speak yer mind and I am sure for a decision such as this, he would ensure to seek yer opinion."

Paige shook her head. "Not always."

Duin was not of good temperament. He made harsh noises to announce his displeasure at being taken away from where he'd found a crop of tasty grasses to munch.

Once he was saddled, she guided the now calmer horse forward to where the party had been joined by her father and Lady Mackenzie. Merida fortified herself and lifted her chin. Upon meeting her father's gaze, she found strength and a silent message that he expected nothing less than absolute fortitude from her.

Handing Duin's reins to the guard, she neared her parents, first hugging her mother who whispered well wishes and promises to visit soon and then Paige who joined in wishing her Godspeed.

Lady Mackenzie was warm and obviously thinking the trip was to be a great adventure by handing her a leather-bound book. "To see ye past the long travel."

"Thank ye." Merida gave the woman a wan smile.

When she faced her father, his gaze slid toward where Tristan was. "He has promised to keep ye safe. I know ye are more than capable, Merida, and I do not expect that ye will allow mistreatment. However know that ye can return home at any time."

She wanted to laugh knowing Tristan overheard every word. Instead, she leaned forward and kissed her father's bearded cheek. "I will never stop being a McLeod first."

His eyes twinkled when she straightened.

Upon turning to face her husband, he motioned to the wagon. "Shall we go?" By the tone of his voice, he was resigned to the fact that she'd not be hurried.

Merida turned in the opposite direction and mounted Duin. "Aye, let us go," she called out.

The front gates remained open and, yet, as they crossed out toward the open lands, it felt as if they closed behind her. She didn't look back, afraid to catch a glimpse of her mother crying. Seeing it would break her resolve to remain strong and not allow the dismay and doubt she felt inwardly to show.

Tristan came alongside her. "We will ride all day. Ye may grow exhausted upon yer horse."

Sliding a glance to him, she wanted to roll her eyes. Instead, she lifted a brow. "I rode all the way here, tis the same distance to yer home."

"It will be yer home now. And no, it is a bit further."

She pressed her lips together. It was doubtful anything on another clan's lands would ever feel like home. "What is yer keep called?"

"*Dun Airgid*," he replied, pride evident in the tone. "Tis a large keep, about the same size as the Mackenzie's, with walls on three side and steep fall behind."

"How many people have thrown themselves to their deaths?"

"Why? Are ye considering it?" he teased and she couldn't help but chuckle.

"Nay, I would rather fight than kill myself." She redirected the question. "Silver Fortress, why that name?"

Tristan met her gaze. "It seems to shimmer at sunrise and sunset. It was named that by the villagers."

A flock of birds flew overhead, their loud caws fading as they went. She looked up and let out a sigh. "Why do ye insist on leaving now? Ye did not say anything about it to me last night."

She shifted in her seat, realizing now that perhaps riding after her first time with a man was probably not the best of ideas.

If he noticed, Tristan did not say anything about it. "I have many duties that have been neglected overly long by my spending so much time away."

"Duties that could not wait one more day?"

Just then, a guard motioned to get his attention and Tristan rode ahead.

"WHAT IS HAPPENING?" Tristan said to the guard, who looked up to the trees.

"The birds have become silent."

Tristan followed the man's line of sight. They'd only been on the road for but a few moments. "Let us pick up the pace and ride faster for a while."

The guard nodded and they began traveling faster. Dispatching two guards ahead and flanked by four on each side, the party was relatively safe. Tristan himself rode in a pattern, moving from the front to the back and, on occasion, alongside the party.

When he rode next to his uncle, the older man glanced over his shoulder and then met his gaze. "Have ye considered that yer wife could be uncomfortable after last night?"

His eyes widened and he turned to study the beauty that sat

straight as an arrow upon her mount. She kept her shoulders straight and her gaze forward. If one did not pay attention, she seemed serene without discomfort, but he noted the slight pinch of her brow and almost invisible lines of tension at the sides of her lips.

"Why would she insist on riding that blasted beast?"

His uncle shrugged. "To show strength. Merida is leaving everything she's ever known behind."

"Ian thinks we may be followed," Tristan said, changing the subject. "The quieting of the birds could be our presence, but he does not think so."

When his uncle nodded, the way he tilted his head reminded him so much of his own father that Tristan's throat tightened. "I have been thinking the same. Look forward and to the left. Do ye notice the shifting?"

When Tristan looked, there was a definite change in the lower brush as if the plants had been jostled just recently and were resettling. "Someone alone?"

"That is what I think," Gregor replied. "A scout perhaps."

Tristan considered whether he should send guards to confront the person or wait to see if, perhaps, he would go away. However, if he was keeping up with them while waiting for others, it could prove disastrous.

"How far to McLeod lands from here?"

"Closer than to our own. It must be a McLeod. We travel in between, using the narrow stretch between McLeod and Mackenzie lands."

Tristan nodded. Upon mapping the route, both to there and back, they had remained away from the McLeod border, ensuring to remain on small clan lands or their own.

"If he is a scout, it could be he belongs to a local clan."

They continued on, deciding the smaller clan who claimed the lands was tiny and they would not pose a threat to the party.

The sun was falling when they finally stopped to rest the horses and set up camp. The air had become crisper, however, the day remained pleasant. As much as Tristan hated stopping, his mind kept returning to Merida's condition. He'd not considered that she would be tender after their wedding night.

Nearing his wife who looked after her mount, he placed a hand on her shoulder. "How are ye feeling?"

She didn't reply right away. Her gaze moved down his face to focus on the center of his chest. "I am tired."

"I had not considered that after last night, ye would need a day of rest. Perhaps ye should ride on the wagon tomorrow."

A light blush crept up from her neck. "I will admit to not being comfortable, however, I prefer my horse to a wagon."

He nodded, admiring her candor. "Ye must rest well tonight. I will see about yer mount."

Before she could protest, he took the saddle from the animal and guided it to the water's edge. The beast should have been tired after the long day of riding, but Tristan was surprised when it pranced at the water's edge before walking into it to drink. It kicked in the water, seeming to enjoy the feel of it around its legs. The beast reminded him of his wife. Not one to be judged on appearance alone.

While the horse remained in the shallow edge of the creek, Tristan rinsed his own face, arms and neck. His own mount drank greedily and then meandered to graze, not paying any heed to how far it went.

He eyed Merida's horse and looked to where his was. When Tristan whistled, his horse looked toward him and then reluctantly came closer.

"Duin, come here," Merida stood at the water's edge, hands on her hips. "Get out of the water."

The horse's ears twitched, but it didn't move. Tristan looked from the stubborn horse to its beautiful owner. "Duin," she repeated. This time, the horse took a couple steps deeper into the water until it lapped his knees.

"Should I not have released him?"

Merida dragged her frown from the horse to Tristan. "Nay, he does this to me all the time. He likes water. But if left to his own devices, he will wander away."

At the words, Tristan looked to where his own horse was and it had also gone further away, once again grazing, its tail switching back and forth. "Mine does the same."

Leaving Merida to see about her horse, he stalked to fetch his own.

MERIDA HAD FINALLY succeeded in convincing her stubborn horse out of the water with a carrot and tethered it to a tree nearby.

A hearty bonfire was lit to dispel the chill in the air and everyone sat near it. Hollowed out bread filled with meat and thick broth that had been sent by the Mackenzie's was shared.

Although a bit colder now that the sun had fallen, Tristan sat close to her, his large body a shield from the cold breeze. Too hungry to speak much, Merida ate every bit of her food. The next day, they'd travel straight to the Ross keep and would, in all probability, eat as they went.

She sneaked a glance to her husband, noticing that although he ate and seemed at ease, his gaze moved constantly to the surrounding trees. He was alert and watchful. Four guards patrolled to ensure no one was about, while another six remained with them, but spread out in a calculated circle.

"Ye find something interesting?" Tristan asked.

"I've noticed how the guards are posted and that ye have not stopped keeping watch. Is there something amiss?"

She was surprised when he replied. "Aye, we are being followed. I am not sure if he belongs to yer clan or the clan these lands belong to."

"Have ye sought to seek him out?"

"Aye, but he evaded my guards."

A shiver of apprehension traveled down her spine. Yet despite the troubling occurrence, she was glad he'd trusted her enough to inform her.

"My old bones require that I sleep now." Gregor Ross stood from where he sat just a short distance away.

Tristan watched his uncle go to where he planned to sleep, blankets already rolled out.

"I have met yer uncle before. He came to my home several times," Merida said.

Tristan looked to her. "My uncle is like a father to me. Always has been. Although I cared for my father greatly, there was always a tight bond between me and Uncle Gregor."

"I am sorry about yer father," Merida said, trying to come to grips with why Ethan, her impulsive brother, did what he did. "I wish he remained alive."

Silence stretched and Merida wondered if she should not have said anything. Finally, Tristan stood and held a hand down to her. "Do ye need to relieve yerself before settling for the night?"

She allowed him to help her up and then they walked in silence away from the others so they would have privacy. Tristan stopped and she continued forward to where she could ensure to empty her bladder. After she was done, she found him leaning on a tree, seeming deep in thought.

When she approached, he wrapped an arm around her waist and pulled her against him. The solidness of his frame along with the trickles of awareness that traveled down her body made Merida lift her arms up and around his neck, pulling him down until their lips met. Tristan needed little encouragement, his mouth covering hers and his tongue delving past her lips. She pressed harder into him, needing to feel his body against hers.

Tristan's large hand slid down her backside until cupping her from behind and lifting her until their sexes aligned. Merida moaned at the friction that was brought on by the presence of their clothing.

"Allow me to make love to ye," Tristan said, his voice ragged, hot breaths against her ear. "I need to."

The need was mutual and she clung to him, wrapping her legs around his waist as he maneuvered to free his erection.

She wasn't sure how, but her skirts were moved aside and his staff penetrated in one strong thrust. Thankfully, he muffled her cry with his mouth and continued to cover her mouth as she moaned when a myriad of sensations took over her entire being.

Hard and thick, his manhood filled her to capacity, the walls of her sex stretching to allow the wonderful invasion.

While holding her up against a tree, Tristan was free to move and he pushed into her, sending waves through her body as she did her best to keep from crying out. They didn't have much time, so his movements became frantic, sliding out and delving back in as both sought to find their releases.

Merida's body went rigid as a climax hit so hard, lights flashed before her. Soon after, Tristan groaned and his body shuddered.

They remained entwined, with Merida clinging to him as she waited for her breathing to regulate. As much as she wanted to remain angry at him for dragging her away from her family so soon, tenderness enveloped her when he helped her to stand, taking time to arrange her skirts. He straightened and looked at her hair, then clumsily patted it as if trying to tame the mass of curls.

Merida chuckled. "There is not much that can be done to tame my hair."

"I believe the same goes for my beautiful wife." His eyes seemed to sparkle in the moonlight and Merida wondered how often he would be like this. Allowing his guard down and giving her an insight to the less hardened man.

"We should go back," he said, looking toward the camp. "Come." He placed a hand at the small of her back and guided her toward where the wagon was.

Once at the wagon, he assisted her to join a sleepy Elsa, who sat in waiting. "Would ye like me to brush yer hair, Lady Merida?"

"Nay, we will do it in the morning. I am too exhausted to think about such things and I know ye are as well." They settled into the nest of blankets that had been thoughtfully provided by Lady Mackenzie and her mother. Merida barely noticing where Tristan went.

TRISTAN WENT TO where Ruari sat staring into the fire. "What do ye think? Is the person still following us?"

"Nay, not now. Which is more worrisome."

Tristan nodded. "He could be gone to let others know where we are."

"Sleep now. I will wake someone up to take my place."

"Wake me," Tristan said, unwrapping his tartan and settling onto the ground not too far from the fire.

At daybreak, the party didn't waste time preparing for the day ahead. With luck, they would make it to *Dun Airgid* before sunset.

The horses were prepared for riding; two were hitched to the wagon. Once again, Merida mounted her unruly beast of a horse, looking to be more at ease.

Tristan neared and leaned closer. "Are ye not too tender to ride?"

Although there was a slight coloring on her cheeks, she met his gaze directly. "I will not ride in the wagon, Husband."

They rode off at a steady pace. The thought that perhaps whoever had been watching them had gone off to fetch more men was heavy on their minds. Soon, however, they reached the outskirts of Ross lands.

The road became narrow, forcing them ride in lines of two. An uneasiness stretched as they realized that by doing so, being further apart meant they made an easier target. Although near Ross lands, the area was adjacent to McLeod territory.

Tristan went to ride alongside Merida and instructed a guard to pull Elsa to ride with him.

The air was thick, the silence in the trees ominous.

"What is going on?" Merida asked, noticing how the guards moved to flanks of two, their swords at the ready.

"Just a precaution since we travel along McLeod lands for the next while." Tristan scanned the trees, not seeing anything of interest. It was best to err on the side of caution he conceded. However, the sense of dread did not lift.

The first arrow whizzed right past his head and just as Tristan called out in alarm, a second one hit, lodging into his upper left arm.

He swung his horse around and pulled out his own bow, loading it with an arrow and loosing it to the treetops from where the arrows came.

One of the Ross guardsmen fell to the ground, hitting so hard the air was knocked from him.

A second man fell.

Uncle Gregor.

CHAPTER FOURTEEN

SEVERAL MEN FELL from the trees as Tristan loosed arrow after arrow from behind the cover of trees now. They were McLeods by the tartan colors.

While two guards dragged their injured to safety, he and Ruari dragged his uncle and the other injured man behind the wagon.

Meanwhile, Merida screamed out at the top of her lungs. "Do not attack. We are now in alliance with the Ross." She whirled around, fiery hair loosening from its bindings. "Stop at once. I order it. I am Lady Merida McLeod."

The arrows finally stopped falling and knowing the men were climbing from their perches, Tristan, Ruari and six men rushed toward the trees.

"Do not go," Merida cried out, rushing after them. "They outnumber ye."

Ruari pulled his horse to a stop and his face, twisted in fury, turned toward Merida. "Ye knew this would happen, didn't ye?" He stalked to Merida, whose eyes widened. "Ye meant to have us killed so ye could go home."

"I did not." Merida stood up to the furious man, not shrinking away in the least. "It makes little sense. I did not know about us returning until just moments before we left."

Tristan intervened. "Enough Ruari. We must go see about Uncle Gregor and Fergus," he said, referring to the injured guard.

He didn't take the time to see what happened, if anyone followed. All he knew was that he could not lose his uncle. Not so soon after the death of his father.

Gregor lay on the ground, a guard holding a rag over the wound. He'd been pierced through his abdomen. Gregor's gaze met his. "I will be fine. However, the wagon may be the best way for me to travel forth." He coughed and the rag became bloodier. Tristan did his best to hide his alarm.

"Where's Merida?" He stalked away to find his wife.

She stood next to her horse, stroking its long nose, looking up to him as he approached.

"Why are ye not coming to see about my uncle or Fergus? Ye are a healer, are ye not?"

"I was not sure yer men would want me near," she replied, not seeming upset in the least.

"Come see about them now," Tristan demanded, looking into the wagon. "Where is the healing basket?"

Elsa, her maid, held it up and scrambled down from the back of the wagon. "I will assist my lady."

Just then, guards approached with his uncle who had lost consciousness. Merida and Elsa directed the men to lay him upon a pallet that was laid out quickly. Merida then tore his tunic open and looked at the wound. "Ye should not have pulled the arrow out."

"We pushed it through," one of the men snapped.

She didn't bother answering. Instead, she sent the same man to fetch water and instructed another to roll Gregor so she could peer at the exit wound. Once the water was brought, she rinsed out the wound and packed it with clean cloths. That seemed to thwart the bleeding. His midsection was bound tightly.

Fergus was in better condition; the man sat up, his back against a tree trunk. He'd been struck in the upper chest, but did not seem to be badly injured. Once Merida bandaged him, she turned to Tristan.

"I need to look at yer arm."

It was then that Tristan noticed he was bleeding, the blood seeping through his tunic and dripping to the ground. In his haste to begin shooting arrows back, he'd not noticed the arrow remained. It must have broken off because only a few inches of wood stuck out from his arm.

As if knowing about the injury sent an alarm though his body, pain pierced and he swayed. Thankfully, the warrior in him took over and he let out a breath. "Very well."

He lowered to the tree stump by the fire and pulled his tunic off. He didn't want her tearing it since it was a favorite of his.

Merida studied his wound and pronounced it safe for the arrow to be pushed through. She went back to Gregor while one guard held Tristan by the shoulders and Ruari pushed the arrow through. Tristan groaned at the tearing of flesh, his vision blurring for a moment.

"Gregor remains unconscious," Ruari said, looking worriedly toward where Merida hovered over their uncle.

Tristan's heart thundered as anger filled him. "How can we keep a truce when they continue to attack us? Tis not possible."

"It was what ye agreed to." Merida had approached. "Ye cannot go back on yer word."

"Yer clan did." He stood, no longer caring about the wound. "Yer clan attacked while there was a truce in place. Ye cannot blame it on us this time."

Fire flew from her eyes as she leaned forward to make a point. "Ye could have waited for us to leave. Allowed for father to send a scout to ensure the way would be safe."

"There should not be a need for it. We had a truce before even going to the Mackenzie's." He couldn't help but shout at her. "Ye better pray my uncle does not die. I will ensure every last McLeod is dead."

Merida's eyes rounded. "Whoever it was that attacked has nothing to do with me and my family."

"They were McLeods," he yelled.

Her face red, she stormed closer, poking a finger into his chest. "Obviously, they were not aware of the truce. They would have been the ones my father would have sent word to."

Jaw clenched to keep from yelling further, he growled, "Word should have been sent when the truce was agreed upon, otherwise they wouldn't have broken it."

It became evident that Merida was not about to back down. Tristan understood, on some level, that she was right but, at the same time, he was not wrong in that the McLeod should have sent word to all his people of the truce.

The guardsmen pretended not to be listening, but it was evident by the silence that they were.

Merida looked from him to where her horse was, a sign she thought of fleeing. "I do not take responsibility for anything. It was a choice made by ye without asking me. If given the choice, I would not stand here as yer wife right now."

"And neither would I as yer husband," he answered. "Now, go see about my uncle and ye better pray he lives." He pointed to the man still lying on the ground.

She took a step forward and then turned to regard him. "The truce is over whether or not he lives and we both know it."

They rode faster toward the Ross keep. Although still unconscious, Tristan's uncle clung to life. Merida rode with him in the wagon, her attentions like that of a mother bear attempting to keep him from jostling overly much.

By the time *Dun Airgid* game into view, everyone was exhausted. A party of guards greeted them and immediately escorted them through the gates.

There was activity everywhere, the men helping take his uncle from the back of the wagon and assisting Fergus as well.

The news of the attack soon reached a fevered pitch with everyone demanding they immediately go and seek retribution for what had happened. Tristan followed his cousin into the great room, searching out his brother.

There was much to discuss and not enough time to see about everything at once. He wondered for a moment if perhaps he should go ensure his uncle fared better, but he knew Merida would stay with him and be joined by their healer and Elspeth. Word would be sent to him if anything of note occurred.

Malcolm rushed to him, emerging from the corridor that led to his study. "What the hell happened?"

"We were attacked by McLeods," Tristan replied, his jaw tight. The anger from his argument earlier still coursed through him. "The damn laird must not have sent word to everyone of the truce."

Malcolm's brown gaze moved to a large room near the kitchens. The healer had been sent for and Malcolm's wife, Elspeth, who was herself an expert, had raced by earlier.

"First let us to see about Uncle Gregor. Then we will talk." Malcolm frowned and searched the great room. "What of yer wife? Ye cannot just leave a McLeod unescorted right now."

Tristan turned toward the main entry. There wasn't anyone there. "She may be with Uncle Gregor."

The brothers hurried to the sick room. Once there, Gregor was on one of the beds. On one side of the sick man was their healer and on the other was Elspeth, their heads together as they examined him. Other than that, there wasn't anyone else in the room.

Malcolm met his gaze. "Go see about yer wife. I will remain here."

In the courtyard, the people had dispersed to smaller groups that seemed to continue speaking of what had happened. No doubt, most feared the return of battling. He headed to the stables knowing Merida would be seeing about her beast before seeking him.

"Where is Merida?" he asked Ruari and the stable hands who were unsaddling horses and brushing them down.

"She went with her horse and her maid toward the corral," Ruari said, his attention back to the horse he led to a stall.

Annoyed, Tristan decided she'd come to find him once she did whatever it was she was going to do with the horse. He motioned a lad over. "Go to the corral and watch over Lady Merida. Ensure she is not harmed and bring her directly to the great room once she is done with her horse."

"The McLeod?" the young man asked with a grimace. "'Tis true ye married a McLeod?"

"Go do as ye're told," Tristan snapped. "Now." With a sheepish expression, the lad ran off.

"Are we back at war with the McLeods?" a guard approached and asked.

"I do not know. Once I speak to Malcolm, we will decide."

"If something happens to yer uncle, we cannot let it lay," the man said, eyes forward. "'Tis a shame really."

Tristan looked to the man. "Why do ye say that?"

"I planned to marry later this spring. I will not during time of war. I will not leave a widow."

Understanding the man's point of view, Tristan suddenly wished it would not be so, that his clan would live in peace for a bit longer.

He walked into the keep with trepidation and headed to the sick room. Just as he rounded the corner, Malcolm came out of the doorway.

"Uncle Gregor has woken. He will survive this."

Relief washed over him. "I feel responsible in part. For leaving so hastily."

"'Tis not yer fault the McLeod did not see to it that everyone knew about the truce."

"He asked for time to send scouts ahead." Guilt assailed him at the thought his uncle could have died because of his decisions.

Malcolm seemed to understand. "I know what ye feel."

Once in the great room, the same lad he'd sent to find Merida meandered from table to table, looking under them. Many times, children did it in hopes of finding coins dropped by visitors. Most of the time, the servants found them first.

"Why are ye not fetching Lady Merida?" he asked the boy, who jumped at the sound of his voice.

The boy frowned up at him. "She has gone. My friend, William, said she paid him a coin to show her a different way out of the keep." He must have caught sight of something shiny because he dove under the table, his dirty hands moving rushes aside.

"Ah!" the boy yelled when Tristan lifted him up by the back of his tunic and held him up until they were face-to-face. "Take me to this boy, William, and do not be surprised if ye get a lashing for not finding me right away."

The boy ran to keep up with Tristan as they walked to where a skinny boy sat atop a corral fence, watching the horses. Often, orphans and foundlings were given menial jobs that paid them a coin or two. They were fed and housed in two small cottages Elspeth had built for them.

William's eyes rounded and he scrambled from the fence. Before he could run away, Tristan managed to grab him by his scrawny arm. "Show me where she went." He didn't raise his voice. At this point, he was not only exhausted and hungry, but also wished for nothing more than a bath and his bed.

Being a husband was turning out to be much more troublesome than he could have imagined.

The boy's face brightened and he raced to a corner behind a garden shed. He pointed to rocks that had been stacked and a makeshift ladder. "We made this to go to the village." There was pride in his voice. Obviously, the lads snuck away often to spend their coin and had become prolific in their escape routes. Not that anyone would have stopped them, but Tristan understood the need for adventure.

"What of her horse?"

William shrugged. "I suppose the other lady took it. When she left out the front."

He let out a long breath to keep from yelling at the boys. "Very well. Go on."

Just as he passed the stables, Ruari came out. "Where are ye headed?"

"My wife left." He didn't bother turning around, already grabbing one of the horses a guard led to the stables. "I will return shortly," he said to the man who nodded.

Once at the gates, he mounted and galloped at full speed in the direction of McLeod lands. Not only would he have another loud argument with Merida but, after her actions, he would probably volunteer to take her home himself. Marriage to a McLeod was a mistake and no matter how much his body reacted to her, demanding her near, he had to accept the fact that they were not suited.

A war between the clans would ensue and it was best for her to be with her own clan when it came to pass. An enemy among the clan would make it hard not only for Merida, but for him to defend her when his clan would do anything to harm her.

He could not remain about the keep to guard her. He was a warrior and would be away at battle.

This was all a huge mistake that had to be corrected immediately.

It wasn't long before he spotted the duo. Something had happened. The hellish horse was beside a creek and Merida sat on the ground. Her maid, Elsa, stood by the water's edge wetting a cloth in the water.

Chapter Fifteen

Merida wasn't surprised when the sounds of horse hooves pounding the ground came closer. They were still on Ross lands and had only made it a short distance before she'd noticed throbbing pain at her ankle. She'd tripped when climbing over the wall, but with adrenaline pushing her to get away without notice, she ignored her injury.

After soaking it in the creek's cool water, her ankle felt a bit better, but now it was impossible to walk on it, the pain unbearable.

Elsa hurried to join her, thrusting the wet cloth at her. "For yer face. He comes now." The young woman's eyes moved past her to the approaching Tristan.

By the flare of his nostrils and glare, he was enraged. Good, so was she. How dare he think to leave her unescorted after announcing that her clan attacked? It was a miracle that she'd been able to sneak away when everyone's attention had been drawn by the men carrying Gregor Ross from the back of the wagon. As she'd shrunk back into Duin, men had eyed her and made menacing gestures.

No matter what her husband said or did, Merida had made up her mind. It was best for her to return home.

Tristan dismounted and gestured to Elsa. "Give us some privacy."

Her loyal companion looked at Merida and she nodded. "I will be fine."

The woman went back to the water's edge near to where Duin grazed. The animal lifted its head and looked to the newcomer with what seemed like dislike. Merida wanted to smile.

"Why did ye leave without telling me?" Tristan stood straight, hands to his sides, his darkened eyes meeting hers.

She hitched her chin. "I needed fresh air perhaps." Although it was a dangerous game to needle the already angry warrior, she couldn't help it.

As expected, he wasn't at all amused. "Stand up. We will return home and speak about this."

"No. I will not return there. That is not my home. I left because when war resumes between our clans, I prefer to be with my people."

"War will not be declared." A muscle at his jawline jerked. Merida had to admire his restraint. His voice remained even, his body somewhat at ease.

She let out a breath. "It will be and ye have to admit it. I am already unwelcome, especially after what happened. My being there is a danger to not only me, but Elsa as well. I will not remain and be killed in my sleep."

When he ran his hand roughly down his face, she noticed blood seeping from the bandage on his left arm. "Why did they not sew yer wound shut?"

The sound he made was somewhere between a growl and a groan. "Because I had to leave to find my wayward wife."

Forgetting about her ankle, she shifted sideways and winced. At the expression, he suddenly took stock of her body, noting the fact she'd removed her right shoe.

"What happened?"

"Nothing."

Without another word, he bent at the waist, took her up into his arms and stalked to his mount. When he realized Elsa remained behind, Tristan turned to the stricken woman.

"Can ye ride that beast?"

Elsa nodded. "Sometimes."

"Follow us then."

Despite the pain of being moved, Merida could not ignore the feel of his strong body against her. Immediately, memories of their entwined nude skin touching assailed her and she frowned. This was not a time for romanticism. She had to be strong and change her mind about leaving him.

To her surprise, Tristan held his horse to a slow pace, the animal meandering through the fields. He'd directed that she lift her leg up and onto the animal's neck, which she was sure looked ridiculous, but it helped keep it from swelling further.

Although it was cumbersome to ride slowly, she knew he did it to keep from hurting her further.

"Tristan, we should talk calmly," Merida began. "Neither of us wished for this marriage. However, we are husband and wife…"

"Ye made a vow to obey and be loyal and yet ye left without speaking to me about it." There wasn't a tone of anger now, but more of resentment. Merida's heart tightened.

"Ye are right. But understand that I felt I was in danger and I sought to keep myself and Elsa safe." She looked up at him and their gazes met. Tristan had the most beautiful, thickly-lashed hazel eyes. Admittedly, Merida loved looking at him. He was not handsome in a classic way but was a more masculine, rugged sort.

Finally, Tristan nodded. "Ye should have come and sought me out. Although I'm angry, I am not unreasonable."

Shocking her, he pulled her against him and held her tightly. "What am I going to do with ye?"

After a few moments, Merida couldn't help but relax, allowing his strength to seep through. If it were just the two of them, without clan controversy, without the feud, she would find it very easy to fall in love with this man. However, their situation was much too difficult to traverse. There were too many dividers.

"Ye must allow me to return to my clan," Merida said softly. "Tis for the best."

He grunted, which didn't make it clear to her if he agreed or not, so she continued. "Under different circumstances, I would not object to being yer wife. I think we would be good together..."

"Stop talking." Tristan grunted again. "I am losing blood and will fall off this horse if I don't concentrate on getting us back."

It was then she noticed he was sweating profusely, his face pale. However, his unwavering strength continued to astound her. He pushed the horse to go a bit faster until the keep came into view. Then he made a signal and several men on horseback rode toward them.

"Take her," Tristan said to the first man rode up. "Be with care, she is injured."

Just as she settled against the guard who held her steady, Tristan fell from his horse, hitting the ground with a loud thump.

TRISTAN OPENED HIS eyes to find he was in his bedroom. He immediately sat up and regretted it when the room spun. After a few moments, things stopped spinning and he could look around properly.

Merida sat next to the bed, her right leg propped up onto a stool. She watched him silently.

The healer and Elspeth stood next to the bed. Elspeth smiled at him. "Happy to see ye awake."

It took him a moment to get his bearings, to recall what happened earlier. "How long have I been here?"

His wife was the one to respond, her gaze moving across his bare chest. "It is late in the day. Ye lost a lot of blood." When her eyes moved from the center of his chest to meet his, it was as if she touched him.

Thankfully, the healer cleared his throat and brought their attentions back to the matter at hand. "I suggest ye eat well and rest to gain yer strength..."

"My uncle?" he interrupted the man. "How does he fare?"

Elspeth neared and gave him an understanding look. "He is faring well, has woken and spoke to us. We feel he will recover promptly."

"Ye should be there with him and not here. I do not require attention."

Merida and Elspeth exchanged glances. Tristan couldn't decipher whether they were friends or foes.

Elspeth nodded. "Aye, we have been with him all day. Tis that I had just walked in to speak to Merida when ye woke."

Throwing the sheets away and sliding to the edge the bed, he ignored the fact he was completely nude. "I am well. I have to speak to my brother."

"Be with care when ye stand," the healer said, already heading to the door, a flushed Elspeth behind him. They walked out.

Merida looked down at a book she held, seeming to have already forgotten his presence. But she slid a look to him and then back to the book. "If ye fall, I cannot be of assistance."

Deciding it was best not to make a fool of himself, Tristan stood slowly. The room didn't spin this time, but only swayed a bit. Once he was steady, he sought a clean pair of breeches and a tunic.

When he was finally fully dressed, he studied Merida for a moment until she raised her gaze to him.

"Has last meal been served?"

"Nay, tis not that late as yet."

"I must speak to my brother. Ye and I will talk later."

A strange chasm had materialized between them and he wished it would disappear. She didn't seem inclined pay him any mind. Quite the opposite, she had a calm appearance. His heartbeat picked up at the thought of reaching for her.

"Would ye send Elsa in please? She should be outside the door."

Tristan nodded. In the hallway, sitting on a chair, was Merida's companion. She immediately stood at seeing him, her eyes wide.

"Yer mistress requires ye," Tristan told her. "I will send a servant with food for ye both."

"Thank ye," the meek woman said, scurrying around him and into the room, slamming the door behind her.

Once he spoke to Malcolm and saw how his uncle fared for himself, he would make a final decision about what to do with Merida. She was his wife and the protector in him raged that he should not forsake her at any time. However, would it be more dangerous to keep her by his side?

At the bottom of the stairs, servants hurried to and fro preparing for last meal. He hated to have lost the entire day, especially if his brother had made decisions regarding what would happen next.

With only a few sconces that held candles for light, the dimness of the hallway seemed to help keep Tristan steady as he made his way to the sick rooms.

Inside the sparse room outfitted with only a bed, two chairs and a table, he found his brother seated next to the bed. In it, his uncle had been propped up with pillows. He remained pale, but his gaze seemed clear. His uncle and brother spoke in low tones and Tristan took a moment to study them.

Malcolm wore the title of laird well, his sense of honor always at the forefront. The formidable warrior had settled easily into the task of lording over the clan. Although not prepared for the sudden death of their father, he lorded over the clan with fair and impartial decision-making.

As long as Tristan could remember, Uncle Gregor had been an advisor to the clan. Without him, surely they would be adrift. His uncle's resemblance to his father was astonishing and, while comforting at times, it made it harder to accept the loss of his father.

The men stopped talking when his uncle looked to the door. When their gazes met, it was as if his uncle read his mind. "I am well and will recover. I do not plan to leave ye or yer brothers anytime soon."

Tristan nodded, unable to form a sentence. Malcolm looked him over from head to feet and back up. "Are ye well enough to be about?"

"I am not a child…" Tristan began, but had to stop when the room went sideways and he had to lean on the doorway for support. "We need to talk."

His brother stood and motioned for Tristan to sit. "Aye, we do. This attack…how did they know ye would be traveling through the area. From what Uncle says, the road ye took was not the usual way."

Tristan sat in the chair Malcolm emptied. "Aye, we never traveled on McLeod lands. I ensured it. I believe someone got word out. Possibly a McLeod who is unhappy with the marriage."

Malcolm let out a loud breath. "No one is dancing with joy at the joining of our clans. I certainly doubt yer new bride is since she ran off the first chance she got."

Tristan felt the need to defend his wife. "Merida realizes there may never be peace between our clans and prefers to return to her home and family."

It surprised Tristan when his uncle also defended Merida. "The lass is not a weakling. She is a strong, independent lass. However, she is intelligent as well and would not do anything to start another clan war."

"Are ye going to allow her to leave then?" Malcolm studied him, as if searching for something other than what Tristan would state.

"I am not sure. A part of me agrees that perhaps she would be better off returning to her clan. However, there is the possibility that she could be with child. I will never allow my child to live with them."

Both turned when Gregor chuckled, his eyes already drooping with fatigue. "I had not considered that."

Malcolm frowned. "We will not go to war. I have decided against it and our uncle agrees. What I do plan to do is to find out who is responsible for the attack."

"It could be anyone. The McLeod himself could have ordered it, but I doubt he would ever put Merida in that kind of danger," Tristan replied.

"Nay, he would not allow for arrows to rain down in the way it was described to me," Malcolm said. "Merida could have been killed."

There was a knock on the door and a guard walked in. "Laird, a messenger has arrived. He comes from Laird McLeod."

"Escort him to the great room." Malcolm stalked to the doorway and Tristan stood to join him. His brother looked to their uncle. "I am grateful that ye will be well. I will return to speak of whatever this messenger has to say."

Their uncle waved them off, his eyes already closing.

"Is the healer sure he will recover fully?" Tristan asked his brother as soon as they were out of Gregor's earshot.

"He assures me it is so." Malcolm continued on down the corridor and into the great room where two guards escorted a young man whose wide eyes moved from taking in the large room to them and back around to his two escorts.

"Laird," the messenger said upon seeing Malcolm. "I bring…"

"Give me a moment," Malcolm interjected and motioned for those in the room to leave. Servants hurried out.

Once they were alone with only Malcolm's personal guards, the messenger was allowed to speak.

"My laird wishes to meet and talk."

"Is yer laird aware of the attack on the party by McLeods upon returning from the Mackenzie's?" Malcolm asked.

The messenger frowned. "Nay, I do not believe so. Is Lady Merida injured?"

Tristan studied the young man. "She is not." He preferred to not disclose the ankle injury.

"We will meet with yer laird in neutral territory," Malcolm said, his gaze pinpointing the messenger. "Kildonan, the village just past Loch Broom."

"I will inform my laird."

"Has he returned home?" Tristan asked.

"Aye, he was on the way home when he dispatched me here."

Malcolm waited a few beats, obviously considering what else to ask. "Do ye know what yer laird wishes to discuss?"

"I do not."

"Have ye spoken to Ethan?" Tristan asked next.

"Nay, I have not." It was admirable how the young man did not seem at all discomfited by their questioning. Instead, it was as if he expected to be questioned.

"I believe my laird sent him off to see about the northern borders," the messenger volunteered, knowing it would be virtually impossible for a Ross to travel through McLeod lands to reach their northern borders.

Malcolm tensed and immediately Tristan realized for whom it would not be impossible. Kieran was at the northernmost post. At the edge of Ross lands. If their younger brother found out about Ethan's whereabouts, he would not hesitate to seek revenge.

Having left before Tristan's marriage, Kieran had no way of knowing. It wasn't the consequences with the McLeod they feared, but the possibility of Kieran being injured. Ethan McLeod was without honor and would not hesitate to kill Kieran.

That the McLeod asked to meet could be another attempt to plea for Ethan's life. It was possible the man would seek the safety of his youngest son.

"Go to the kitchens and make sure ye are fed before returning to yer laird. We will meet with him at midday in three days." Malcolm looked to his guards. "Two of ye remain with him and make sure he is not harmed."

After the messenger left, servants meandered back into the great room to prepare for last meal. Tristan and Malcolm moved away to the large hearth.

"We have the advantage of visibility," Tristan said, considering that they'd travel from higher land to the meeting place.

Malcolm nodded. "They have the advantage of seeing us approach as well." His brother studied him for a moment. "It could be a good time to return yer bride if ye wish."

"True." Tristan looked into the fire. "What should I do?"

"As ye said, if there is a possibility of a bairn, tis best for yer wife to remain. Either way, ye made a vow, Brother."

"It will be difficult for her. With our recent clan wars, she will have little protection when I am not about."

Malcolm's lips curved. "I would not say that. Elspeth has taken a liking to her and has ensured every servant is informed that yer wife is to be respected."

"Is that true?"

"Aye," his brother said, nodding. "Do not underestimate our women. I assure ye that within days, Merida will be part of this clan."

Malcolm didn't know his wife and Tristan wasn't so sure Merida would be as compliant as his brother expected.

"I will be at last meal. First, I must see about her horse. The beast is unfriendly." He stalked out to the courtyard, glad to notice everything continued as before. Those that were there did not look to him with any kind of animosity.

Horses grazed in the corrals, their tails swishing back and forth in the cooling breeze. Tristan walked into the stables and found that Duin remained in a stall.

"Ruari? Are ye here?"

His cousin called out from the back. "Aye."

"Has Merida's horse been out?" he asked, walking to where his cousin lay on a cot.

"Nay, the beast does not allow anyone near. It took me and four guards to get him into the stall."

Tristan went back to Duin's stall and studied the animal that shook its head as if in warning. "I know ye like to be outdoors, so come along."

He reached around the horse's neck to pull on the reins that remained around his head. "Come now." He slowly opened the stall door, not looking away from the horse.

Other than pawing the ground, the animal exited the stall as meek as a tamed mare. He followed Tristan outside.

"Well, that is something I didn't expect," Ruari said as he joined Tristan while he removed the bridle and loosed the animal into the corral.

"I think he recognizes me now. I do not trust him enough to ride him however."

Tristan looked to the keep. "A messenger came from the McLeod. He wishes to meet. We go in three days. Would ye come with us?"

Ruari nodded. "What do ye think he wishes to speak about?"

"The conditions of the truce. He may request that we not kill his youngest son."

Ruari grunted. "We will never allow that bastard to live."

"We will not," Tristan agreed.

CHAPTER SIXTEEN

PAIGE ROLLED AWAY from Alec and he pulled her against his chest, enjoying the feel of her plush body against his. They were spent after making love. Everything felt right once he was beside her.

"I missed ye terribly," she murmured. "The days were so long."

"The nights longer," Alec replied, nuzzling her neck.

Once she fell into an exhausted sleep, Alec remained awake. He couldn't rest thinking of his sister. Merida was no longer under their protection. And although it had been expected that she'd marry soon and live elsewhere, he'd never even considered she'd be living with their enemies.

With each hour that passed, he worried more about her. Thankfully, his father had agreed to request a meeting with the Ross. This way, they could be made aware of how Merida fared and also ensure that Malcolm and Tristan became aware that Clan McLeod would take her back without any questions or repercussions.

He should be sleeping deeply. After a day of seeing to clan needs and riding to visit a nearby farmer, he'd barely had time to settle before his parents and wife returned from Mackenzie lands.

The evening meal had seemed to last forever so that he'd barely been able to resist dragging Paige from the main hall to have some privacy. Finally upon entering their chamber, they'd made love, talking between each time about what the other had missed.

He admired his beautiful wife and the position she'd quickly gained at the keep. Although she was from a humble background, Paige had managed the household admirably along with his mother. Not only had she ensured all ran efficiently, but also she'd garnered the respect of the servants by being fair but unbending.

He slipped from the bed and, after wrapping his tartan about his body, went down to his father's study. Sitting at his desk was his father with a glass of whisky in his hand.

The McLeod looked up as he entered. "Ye cannot sleep either," his father stated the obvious. "What keeps ye up?"

"Thoughts of Merida. Of Ethan."

His father chuckled. "Already stepping into my shoes." He drank from the glass. "Merida will be well. I noticed Tristan Ross was already smitten with the lass."

"What of my brother."

"He will not live long, Alec. We must accept it."

LADY MCLEOD ENTERED the room just as Paige finished pinning her hair up. The woman had dark circles under her eyes and, yet, remained attractive. "I am glad to be home," Lady McLeod said nearing. "Although I'm thankful for the reprieve of being inside the keep, I missed everything."

Paige smiled herself, glad to see the woman. "I missed it as well. Did ye not sleep well?"

"I am horribly worried about Merida. I wish to ask that either Alec or Clyde go see about her at once," she said, referring to her son and husband.

Paige stood and reached for her mother-in-law's hand. "I will join ye in requesting it be so. Although I don't think we will have a hard time convincing them. Alec was up most of the night."

Lady McLeod nodded. "Clyde as well."

Together, they descended the stairs to find the great room already filled with people eating and talking loudly, most glad to have the laird back in their midst.

Alec was with guardsmen by a rear door and did not notice her entrance. She noted the men paid close attention to whatever he said, their faces solemn.

"What do ye suppose they speak of?" Paige asked Lady McLeod who also watched her son. "It seems serious."

"Aye, it does."

After taking their places at the high board, Alec finally joined them. He sat between her and the laird and immediately began speaking with his father. "Word has been sent to him. It may take a day or two."

It was difficult to know what they spoke of and she knew it was not the time nor the place to question her husband about his conversation with the laird. Instead, she'd wait to see what Lady McLeod had gleaned. She would definitely ask Alec once they were alone in their bedchamber.

THAT EVENING, PAIGE went to the gardens just outside the kitchen, as was her custom after last meal. Although she would have preferred helping with cleaning up of the meal, Rose, the cook, did not allow it.

Instead, she was content to oversee the late day weeding of the garden and whatever tasks needed to be done in the small hut that stored herbs. Just as she exited, she noticed a young man entering through the gates. She recognized him as the messenger and immediately her heart lurched. Like him, her brother had gone to take a message to the Ross. Unlike this young man, her brother did not return.

She waited for him to near. "Please, come inside and eat."

When he met her gaze, his lips curved. "I was fed well at the Ross Keep, Lady Paige. But I will eat again once I speak to my laird."

"Ye bring back word of Merida?" She followed him, knowing he was not supposed to give her any word prior to speaking to the laird. The young man hesitated and met her gaze.

"She is well." He continued on and Paige followed, much too curious to remain outdoors.

"There ye are." Her father-in-law motioned the messenger over. Immediately, Lady McLeod entered the room and hurried to her husband's side, ignoring his pointed look.

"Is my daughter as well?" Lady McLeod asked by way of explanation. "I care only to know how she is."

"How fares my daughter?" the laird asked.

"She is well, Laird. The Ross informed me she turned an ankle, but otherwise is unhurt. I did see her as I left. She waved from the window and called out for me to tell ye she loves and misses ye both."

Lady McLeod sniffed. "How did she hurt her ankle? Was her coloring…"

"I do not know, they did not say. However, when I saw her, she looked perfectly healthy, Lady McLeod," the young man replied.

"Is there anything else ye wish to know, Wife?" Laird McLeod looked to his wife and then to Paige. "As ye hear, Merida is well."

"Thank ye," Lady McLeod said to the messenger and relaxed when Paige slipped her arm through hers. Together, they went back toward the kitchens.

Once they were alone, Paige hugged her. "I am happy to hear Merida is well. I fear she must be so alone."

"Aye," Lady McLeod said with another sniff. "My girl is strong, but to be there, surrounded by people who dislike her, could be unbearable."

"Once things settle, we can ask to go visit," Paige said, hoping it was possible.

ALEC AND HIS father waited for the women to depart before asking the messenger to finish.

"The Ross agrees to meet three days hence at Kildonan, the village just past Loch Broom."

The area was familiar to Alec, and he understood why they'd chosen it. It was neutral territory and neither would have full advantage over the other as the village was in the center of flat lands.

"We will see them coming from over the crest when they arrive," his father said thoughtfully. He motioned to the messenger. "Did ye truly see my daughter?"

"Aye, she was at the window. As I said, she looked well."

Alec spoke next. "Who was in the room when ye delivered the message?"

"The two brothers, Malcolm and Tristan." The messenger seemed to mull his next words. "They were not unpleasant to me in the least. They invited me to eat before leaving."

"Anything else?" Alec's father asked.

"Something troubling, Laird," the messenger frowned. "They asked if ye were aware the party returning from the Mackenzie's lands was attacked by McLeods. Tis where I believe yer daughter hurt her ankle. They also asked about Ethan's whereabouts."

Tension fell over Alec's shoulders and he knew his father felt the same.

"Attacked? Did they say where exactly this happened?"

"On the southern border of Munro lands, Laird."

His father stalked across the floor, his hands clenched. "Word must have not gone out to that area. I knew something like this could happen, but Tristan did not give me time to send scouts everywhere."

Alec motioned for one of the guards to come forward. "Get four men and go to the northern villages. Ensure everyone is aware of the truce between us and the Ross."

The guard's face turned to stone. "Aye."

Before he could step away, Alec placed on hand on the man's shoulder. "George, I am aware of how much ye have lost because of this. However, all blame is not with the Ross. Most of it is with our own."

The guard nodded. "I will go see about preparing the men. I will return once we are ready."

Laird McLeod let out a long breath. "The Ross' would never give up on seeking revenge."

Studying his father's stern profile, Alec understood. If anyone killed his father the way Ethan had theirs, he, too, would not rest until the culprit was dead. "What did ye say regarding Ethan?"

"That he was out inspecting the northern borders. As ye told me to say." The messenger let out a breath. "That was all that was asked."

When the messenger left the room, his father collapsed into a chair. "I grow tired of all of this. The days of peace will not return to us. Not for a long time to come."

THE PARTY OF guards departed soon after and Alec stood above the main gate, his mind awhirl. All he could hope for was that the meeting with the Ross would go well. His family needed peace and it would not come until they came to a permanent understanding.

A lone horseman appeared in the horizon and he immediately recognized his brother. Ethan was supposed to be gone for at least a fortnight. His presence in the area did not bode well for their plans.

As usual, his brother cared little about anyone but himself and Alec was sick of it. He motioned down to the guards at the gate. "See that his horse is taken and he is brought to my father's study immediately. I do not care if it is by force."

He raced down the walkway to the keep and down the stairwells until reaching the main floor. Once there, he went to find his father.

Laird McLeod looked up from where he sat looking over a map of the area. "What is it?"

"Ethan has returned."

His father blew out a breath. "Why can that son of mine not do what he is told just once?" He stood, but Alec motioned for him to sit.

"The guards have been instructed to bring him here directly." No sooner did he speak the words than Ethan stormed into the room, four guards behind him. His chest lifted and lowered as he glared first at Alec and then at his father.

"I thought I was returning home, not to the abode of an enemy. I demand to know why I am treated like this," Ethan screamed. "This is my home, is it not?"

"Sit down!" Clyde McLeod had had enough. "Shut up and sit."

Seeming taken aback for a moment, Ethan walked to the nearest chair, but he did not sit. "What is the meaning of this?" He motioned to the four guards who remained at the door.

Alec closed the distance between them coming almost nose to nose with his brother. "Ye have caused nothing but trouble. The loss of many lives and the reason for us to not have peace for months and now ye have the gall to act offended?"

Using both hands, Ethan shoved Alec away. "I do as I please. This is not only a war between Ross' and us. Right now, it seems as if my own family turns against me."

Their father stood and glowered at Ethan. "Aye, ye do as ye please and because of it, we are left to fight to make things right for our people. Do ye even think of them?"

Ethan's nostrils flared. "The Ross deserved to die. He looked down his nose at me as if I were nothing. He was not ever our friend."

His brother was making little sense. Alec shook his head. "Why did ye return? There is much to do to ensure our borders are secure."

"Because I can. I am not some servant to be sent off to do menial work." He sneered at Alec. "I was sent away to keep me out of the way. I know that."

The guards bristled as they often were sent to secure the borders. Alec wanted to slap his brother across the face. "Tis my task as well. Securing the borders is a duty."

"Ye will remain in yer chambers. The door will be locked," their father said, sounding exhausted. "If ye try to leave at any time, I will have ye thrown in the dungeon."

Ethan stalked to where their father stood. "I will not."

Before his brother could react, Alec yanked Ethan's sword from the scabbard and held it to his brother's throat. He motioned to the guards. "Take him and put him in the room downstairs. Make sure the door is locked."

Making an animalistic noise, Ethan threw himself at Alec and punched him in the stomach. The guards immediately grabbed Ethan, taking the struggling man out the door.

"Go down the back stairwell," Alec instructed, following them to the corridor. He hoped to spare his mother from seeing how mentally unstable Ethan had become.

"I will kill ye both!" Ethan called out. "I swear it."

"He is not well," his father stated the obvious and Alec nodded in agreement.

"I will go speak to him."

Alec followed the sounds of Ethan swearing to the cellar where they had two cells that were rarely used. They'd not taken any prisoners in years. The only people who'd inhabited the space were a couple of unruly drunks who'd brawled in the great room.

Ethan turned to face him and pointed at his bloody lip. "Ye see, even the guards have no respect for me. Tis yer fault."

Ignoring his brother's remark, Alec neared the bars of the cell. "If ye would stop acting like ye're mad, perhaps we can discuss things…"

"I am not mad. I am the only person in this family who makes sense. All of ye want peace above all, even self-respect. I will not drag myself before a Ross like a dog."

How had he not seen it before? Ethan was unstable. His gaze remained unfocused as he paced from one end of the cell to the other. "I will get free and kill each and every one of them."

"Why?"

The question stopped Ethan in his tracks and he whirled around to face Alec. "Because I hate them. I abhor them."

"That I know of, a Ross has never done anything to ye."

"That is where ye are wrong." Ethan laughed. "Kieran Ross took everything that mattered from me. He stole it." Once again, he chuckled. "So I took what mattered most to him."

Alec couldn't believe what he was hearing. "Is this about the tournament? Are ye going to tell me that everything, the deaths, the war?" He hesitated, unsure of what was about to be disclosed. "It is all about losing a tournament?" Blood rushed through his body, a thundering whoosh in his ears as fury took hold. If not for the bars, Alec would have attacked Ethan.

"Ye have no idea. It is not as simple as that," Ethan said calmly. "The price of my dignity is high."

"Ye fool. Ye utterly disgusting fool." Alec could not stand to look upon Ethan any longer. "Ye deserve to be whipped."

Ethan neared the bars, a wide grin splitting his face. "And yet, ye and Da will ask that they not pursue me. That they not seek to kill me." He turned away. "That bothers ye, does it not, Brother? It upsets yer hypocritical code of honor."

"Of which, ye have none."

"My code is the only one that makes sense. It is the code of justice. And mark my words, I will ensure Kieran Ross pays dearly for what he did. I will not be made a fool of."

Alec growled. "It was ye who did that. Going about boasting about how ye would win and placing bets. If ye lost, it was not because of anything Kieran Ross did but because ye spent the nights wenching and drinking instead of at practice."

"He cheated!" Ethan screamed. "The bastard cheated."

It was no use to argue with a deranged man. Alec studied Ethan for a moment. "Consider things, Ethan. Acknowledge that ye are on a path that will only destroy ye."

Ethan's unfocused gaze met his. "No, Brother. I will be the victor."

Chapter Seventeen

"May I come?" Merida sat at the dressing table and met Tristan's gaze in the mirror.

"Nay, tis not safe."

"They are my family. If I am present, they will not attack…"

"It did not stop them last time." He neared and shivers of awareness ran down her spine. They had not made love since arriving. Merida knew he was waiting for her to allow it and although, at times, the urge to reach for him was strong, a part of her held back.

He placed a hand on her shoulder. "I do not seek to keep ye from seeing yer family. If ye wish, I will extend an invitation for yer mother to visit."

Merida nodded. "That would be nice. I, however, insist on coming along."

"No." Tristan returned to stand by where he'd pleated his tartan on the floor. Wearing only a tunic, he lay upon the fabric and pulled the belt around his waist. When he got to his feet, the folds fell perfectly past his knees. "Do not be cross with me," he said, turning to her. "Tis best ye remain here. Yer foot is not yet healed properly."

Understanding it was best not to argue, Merida sighed. "How is Duin?"

Tristan visibly relaxed. "He is well. He has not allowed anyone to ride him, but he does allow me to take him from the corral to the stall and back."

It astounded Merida to hear that her horse seemed to trust Tristan. Then again, being male, it was possible the beast sensed that Tristan and she were bound to one another. "Thank ye."

"Do not thank me. I know how important the beast is to ye." Tristan neared and bent at the waist. "Be well, Wife." His lips pressed against the side of her cheek, just far enough to make her wonder why he didn't kiss her on the lips. Every time he kissed her, it was on her cheek.

"Tristan?" she asked, meeting his gaze. "We are married."

He frowned. "Aye, I know."

"Why do ye only kiss me on the cheek?"

When his lips twitched, heat rushed to her face. "What I mean is…"

"No reason really," he said. "I want to ensure ye are comfortable with me."

It made little sense. They'd been intimate, had joined as man and woman. And yet, she understood what he meant. They had much to work out between them. She'd hurt him by her attempt to escape.

Merida stood, ensuring not to place too much weight on her right foot. "Kiss me."

Ever so slowly, his arms came around her and when his lips covered hers, it felt so new, as if they'd never kissed. He tasted of raw masculinity, a mixture of fresh forest and warm fire. Grasping his tunic, she fell against him, allowing his large body to shield her completely.

Tristan broke the kiss and peered down at her. "I find it hard to stop. Tis best I go." Once again, he pressed his lips to hers, this time in a light peck.

The thud of the closing door made Merida realize she remained rooted to the spot. Her husband's effect on her was all-encompassing.

THE TRIP TO Kildonan was half a day's ride. The weather was perfect, the sun accompanied with a cooling breeze. Already, trees were becoming laden with ripening fruits and flowers bloomed, coloring the land with bright hues of purple and yellow.

Tristan and Ian rode in the front. Although the muscular guard had lost his left arm during battle, he'd insisted on returning to duty. After months of training, Ian was once again an able-bodied warrior who remained formidable during swordplay.

Behind them were Malcolm and his four guardsmen and bringing up the rear was Ruari and another three men.

Two scouts had ridden ahead and a group of archers had traveled separately as well. Archers were normally invisible unless one looked. However, in this case, there were not many trees in the area where the meeting would take place which meant the archers would remain in plain view above buildings and on horseback.

As they descended to the village, the opposing clan became visible. The McLeods were on horseback, formed in a similar way as them. Four guards flanked the McLeod and his son, then another group of six men a few feet behind.

The men remained outside of the village near the loch's shoreline. Tristan turned to look at his brother, whose gaze met his before moving to where the McLeods awaited.

At about twenty feet from the McLeod party, Malcolm lifted a hand to signal his group to stop.

"Tristan, Ruari and Ian, come with me."

The four rode forward in silence. Tristan met Malcolm's gaze. "They did not bring archers."

"I noticed." Malcolm's gaze traveled over the tops of nearby trees.

"Our men are here."

"Aye."

Ruari huffed. "They brought more guards that we did."

Upon their nearing, the McLeod dismounted and so did Alec. Their guards remained behind.

Following suit, Tristan and Malcolm, along with Ruari and Ian, did the same.

"My wife lived near here," Clyde McLeod said by way of greeting. He looked to Tristan. "Merida also visited here on occasion."

"I am surprised she and my wife had not met before then," Malcolm said. "Elspeth is from Kildonan."

There was a beat of silence. However, it was not uncomfortable nor did Tristan sense any kind of tension from either the McLeod or Alec.

Dispensing with greetings, the McLeod let out a breath. "I asked to meet with ye since we are now joined by my daughter and yer brother having wed. As ye know, it was not something either of us expected."

Malcolm nodded. "Aye, I am aware. Although I am sure the Mackenzie had his reasons for demanding it, the marriage does not make things between us easier."

"Aye. Which is why I wished to meet and talk."

Tristan looked to Alec, who cleared his throat. "We were not aware of the attack. Messengers have been dispatched to the far villages to ensure all are told of the marriage."

Clyde McLeod lifted his eyes to Malcolm. "Does our truce stand?"

The muscle on the side of Malcolm's jaw bunched. A sign he did not like the McLeod having taken control of the conversation. "There was a truce before the marriage. Why did the attack happen? Surely, ye are aware any attack by yer people would cause war between us again."

"Our truces have been tentative at best."

"A truce is a truce."

"Will ye tell me then that every member of yer clan near and far are kept abreast of what happens between our clans?"

Malcolm huffed in annoyance. "What is done is done. The truce will stand."

Tristan interrupted. "Yer son, Ethan. Is he aware of the truce? Could it be that he may be responsible for the attack?"

The McLeod met Alec's gaze for a moment, a silent communication that was easy to decipher. They were not happy with Ethan.

"My brother is under control. We are ensuring he can cause no more harm." Alec let out a breath. "Neither Father nor I are now nor have ever been in agreement with what Ethan did."

"Killing my father, ye mean?" Malcolm gritted out. "Aye, I am aware. However, that did not stop him from ordering an attack on our small party heading to yer keep at yer request."

When the McLeod did not reply, Malcolm continued. "In both cases, my uncle could have died. He is in bed with an injury after the last attack. Tristan almost died as ye are aware from the earlier attack."

The McLeod let out a sigh. "I am aware. Other than to tell ye that Ethan is confined and, as of now, can cause no more harm, I cannot offer ye more."

They'd reached an impasse. Tristan waited to know what else the McLeod wanted to discuss.

The man met his gaze. "Since the marriage was neither yer decision nor mine, we are open to receiving my daughter back to our family. She does not have to stay with ye. We know it can be troubling for not only yer people, but also for her to remain with the clan we've battled with."

His stomach clenched but Tristan did his best not to show any emotion. Instead, he looked to the man before him. Clyde McLeod was a fair man. Although instinctively, Tristan felt that Alec would be a stronger leader once he became the laird, it did not diminish the man's authority.

"My wife will remain with me."

"What of yer family? Yer clan? Do they wish her to remain there? Can ye guarantee her safety?"

Malcolm slid a glance to him. "My family will come to accept Merida as a member. She is my brother's wife, and both have vowed to be together."

Meeting Alec's regard, Tristan spoke to him. "I will do what I can to keep her safe. I promise ye that."

The younger McLeod shook his head. "Ye cannot make that promise and keep it. There are too many enemies between us."

The truth of the words sunk like daggers into Tristan's stomach, but he refused to acknowledge it. "Yer mother is welcome to visit. Merida wishes to see her. We can send escorts to keep them safe."

The McLeod nodded. "I will consider it and send a messenger."

"Anything else?" Malcolm asked.

"Ye have liberty to pass on McLeod lands to travel to yer northern posts. As I have stated, word has been sent to every village about our truce." He looked to Tristan. "Tell my daughter that all is well and her mother sends her love."

Malcolm narrowed his eyes. "That yer youngest is contained is not enough of a punishment for what he did."

"I understand," the McLeod said. "One day, when ye have bairns, ye will understand how difficult it can be."

When Tristan huffed, Alec looked to him. "We will do our best to keep him ensconced within the keep."

Tristan was not convinced. "We shall see. If he is ever found, we will not hesitate to kill him."

The McLeod held up a hand. "I am appreciative that ye met with us."

The men walked back to their horses and mounted. Each party then headed back the way they came. Tristan did not wish to speak. If anything, he wanted to gallop away and not deal with the questions his brother would bring once they were out of earshot.

As he and Malcolm rode away, Ian and Ruari stayed behind, ensuring the archers would remain in place for a few moments longer before returning back to Ross lands.

"Tis true, ye know?" Malcolm finally said. "Ye cannot guarantee her safety. Perhaps it would be best that she returns to her home."

Tristan kept his gaze forward. "Would ye send Elspeth back home?"

"I do not know. If she was in any danger, it would be hard to keep her exposed to it."

"What can we do?"

"Mother and Verity will return soon. They are already unfriendly to Elspeth who is not our enemy. I imagine it will be worse for Merida." Malcolm turned to him. "And then there's Kieran."

Their brother would not hesitate to show his hatred to Merida. Tristan wasn't sure a person existed that hated the McLeods more than his younger brother.

"He needs to be told prior to returning."

"Aye, he does."

Thankfully, Malcolm didn't persist in speaking on the matter. There were too many emotions going through Tristan's mind. He could not force his wife to remain based on the fact that he'd begun to feel something for her. He'd vowed to keep her safe and every moment at his home was putting her in a dangerous situation.

"When is Kieran due to return?"

"A fortnight."

"Hopefully, we will know if she is with bairn by then. If not, I will give her the option to return home."

Malcolm lifted a brow. "Does that mean ye will not join with her?"

"I have not since returning."

"I am sorry, Brother."

The words were like sinking into an icy loch until every limb was frozen, without feeling. "I am as well. However, what must be done will be."

The rest of the ride, Tristan was silent. Ruari, Ian and Malcolm discussed clan issues and matters that had to be taken care of, seeming to relax as they traveled closer to home.

For Tristan, however, each step closer to home meant he'd have to face the fact that he and Merida would not be together. Upon arriving, he would move out of their shared chamber and ask the servants to inform him when her monthly flows came.

Letting out a breath, he watched a flock of birds heading for trees where they'd settle for the night and he envied their lack of worry.

DEEP IN HIS thoughts, Tristan barely spoke during the last meal and although Merida gave him questioning looks, she did not ask about the meeting. Upon arriving, he told her that her family had sent their love. However, he did not speak of her possible return home.

It seemed that she'd already formed a bond with Elspeth. The women had entered together, along with Elspeth's good friend, Ceilidh, and Merida's companion, Elsa. It was strange to him that Merida, a laird's daughter, would be comfortable with simple village women, but it showed her caring nature. Unlike his own mother and sister, who'd gone away to visit another clan just to be away from Elspeth, he considered that if Merida remained, she and Elspeth would get along well.

"After the meal, we will speak to Uncle Gregor," Malcolm said.

"No doubt he is anxious to hear what was said," Tristan replied.

Merida tapped his lower arm. "Will we speak about it?"

At her whisper, he turned to her. "Aye, we will. Tis nothing that should have ye worried."

Warriors entered through the back corridor. Dirty from travel, they went directly to sit at the nearest table. As they settled, servants hurried to bring them tankards of ale and plates piled with hot food. The leader, an older man with a graying beard, walked up to the high board. "I bring an urgent request from yer brother."

"What is it?" Malcolm replied.

"Scouts have spotted a large group of fighters from the north. They travel toward our border."

Malcolm's lips formed a tight line. "Eat. We will meet in an hour in my study."

"Tis not surprising," Tristan said. "The warmer weather always comes with those wanting to grow their territory."

"I am almost of a mind to give it to them. But I must think of the villagers. They depend on our protection," Malcolm stated, his tone grave.

It wasn't clear to Tristan what the best solution was. The marauders often attacked unexpectedly. They rarely got away with more than a few goats or sheep. And although they were intent on testing the border region, they'd never won a fight. However, this was troubling. That the group was larger and well-armed meant they were after more than farm animals.

As soon as he finished eating, Tristan stood, deciding it was best to speak to his uncle and then with Malcolm to hear what information the returning warrior had to give.

It was gratifying to find Gregor with more color in his face, his sharp gaze snapping to them over the head of a woman who cleaned his wound. His uncle had a clear view down the front of her bodice that he took advantage of. Upon catching Tristan's raised brow, he winked, a devilish gleam in his eyes.

"Nephews, I wondered how long it would be before ye would come to tell me what happened today."

Malcolm didn't sit. Instead, he paced. "The McLeod asks that we return Merida. He also stated that his youngest son is contained. He gave the impression that Ethan is imprisoned within the keep."

"That will not last," Gregor said, his face contorted with anger. "If anything, it will make him even more dangerous as he will escape with a plan in mind."

Tristan grunted. "I hope he does. My sword awaits him eagerly."

"We agreed to continue the truce and I insisted word be sent out to every person on McLeod lands to let them know of it."

Gregor nodded. "What of ye. Have ye sent scouts to do the same?"

"Aye. It was done at yer arrival from the Mackenzie's."

"Good."

The woman moved away from the bed. She was a pretty, older woman who was obviously interested in more than their uncle's wound. She smiled at Gregor. "I will return later with something warm for ye to drink and fresh bread."

"Thank ye," Gregor replied, his eyes following her as she left. "Bonnie woman."

"What do ye think, Uncle?" Tristan asked.

His uncle gave him an understanding look. "As we discussed before, ye must wait to know if yer wife is with bairn. It will also give ye time to see how she adjusts to life here. It may be that both she and the clan's people surprise ye."

"That, I doubt," Malcolm said.

"Why?" Tristan asked. "Yer wife and mine are already on friendly terms."

Malcolm shrugged. "Tis what I think." He changed the subject and turned back to their uncle. "I am glad ye are recovering. I must now go speak to Alasdair. He brings an urgent message from the northern border. A large group is headed there."

Their uncle's face hardened. "Send an army. Tis time to stop them for good."

Upon entering the study, they were informed by Alasdair and the other warriors of what transpired in the north.

The news from their northern posts was not good. Not only had the one large army been spotted headed to the northern border, but a second group was headed to the northeastern one as well.

Lead guards for both warriors and archers were sent for. Two groups of warriors would be dispatched to each area in the north. One would be headed by Tristan, the second by Ian.

It would be three days of riding to arrive but, thankfully, the groups heading to the northern border did not suspect they'd been spotted and were stopping to rest often.

"Although ye have time to get there, remember that the ones coming from the north will be rested. Do not take the fact ye will outnumber them as a sign the battle will be easy."

Malcolm ran both hands down his face. "This is not something I wish to miss."

"All three of us cannot be gone," Tristan said. "One of us must remain to ensure Da's legacy continues."

The men stood over maps, discussing routes and, soon, they decided that Tristan, along with one hundred men, would go to the northernmost border where the larger attack was imminent. Ian and fifty men would go to the northwestern area.

Once the discussion was completed, they decided to depart the next morning once all the men were assembled.

Tristan made his way up to the bedchamber, mulling over what had to be discussed. He'd had little time to get to know Merida and had no idea how she felt about most things.

Upon entering, he was struck by the beautiful picture of his wife seated before the hearth, brushing out her long, burnished hair. The waves fell to her waist and seemed to shimmer from the reflection of the flames.

She turned to him, her expression expectant. "What is happening?"

It was best to tell her what he knew. Being that he'd be leaving and facing battle, it was possible he'd not return.

"I am going to the northern border. There is a threat from unknown forces. A large number of them head to our villages there."

"When do ye leave?" She put her brush down and stood.

Tristan did not hesitate to close the distance between them and pull her into an embrace. "Tomorrow morning. Once everyone is assembled." He kissed her temple. "I will ask that my things be packed at dawn so to not disturb ye with it now."

It was late. Merida was usually asleep by then, but she'd been waiting for him. No doubt to question him about the meeting with her father and brother.

Tristan tipped her face up. "Ye will remain here for now. Malcolm and Elspeth will keep ye safe from harm. I will also assign ye a personal guard."

"I do not feel threatened. Not inside. However, I have not had the opportunity to go outside since I've been unable to walk properly."

Her eyes moved to his lips and Tristan could not resist. The kiss did not linger as he'd promised himself not to join with her. There was still the decision to be made as to whether she would return to her family.

"Did my father say anything about me being returned?"

Tristan's gut clenched and he wasn't sure how to reply. "Why do ye ask?"

Letting out a sigh, she met his gaze. "Because I know my father and mother and they would rather I return than to be in any danger here."

"He said that ye would be welcomed anytime without ill will to me if ye returned home."

Seeming to mull his words, she pushed away and turned to look into the hearth.

Tristan came up behind her, not quite touching, but a hair's distance. "Do ye wish to go home?"

"Aye, I think I do."

CHAPTER EIGHTEEN

IN HER MIND, Merida had considered herself prepared for how she'd feel upon telling Tristan she wanted to leave.

To inform him she wished return home and relieve him of the vows of marriage should have been easy. However, upon the words being said, in her heart, she realized she could not go through with it.

There were more reasons to leave than to remain. The obvious reason to stay was the fact she was married. She had vowed to become Tristan Ross' wife for life.

Now, the formidable warrior stood in the room, seeming to shrink the space with his size. He stood as still as a statue as he digested what she'd said.

Quickly, Merida attempted to explain and let out along breath. "I do wish to return home, but I am not sure I can. I feel strongly about our marriage and the vows we made."

He slid a glance to her and she wondered what he was thinking. How she wished to know him better and understand every nuance of his expressions.

And yet in her heart, she understood that her words had hurt him. Although he did not wish for the marriage from the start, her wishing to leave remained a rejection.

"Tis not ye that I reject, Tristan, but the fact I will never be accepted."

"There has not been enough time," he replied and went to the bed. He unwrapped the tartan from his body and climbed into bed. "Once I return, we will see."

Did he mean to send her back? Merida went to the bed and climbed up and sat atop the bedding. "What do ye mean? See about what?"

"Merida, I am tired. I have to get up early." Tristan rolled away from her.

She tapped his shoulder. "How long will ye be gone?"

"A fortnight, perhaps longer."

Her heart sank. How was she to remain there for so long alone? Merida scrambled closer and peered over his shoulder. His eyes were closed, but she knew he was awake. "That is a long time."

He did not reply.

"I could return home while ye are gone and come back when ye return."

"No."

"That is unreasonable," she snapped. "What if someone kills me? How will ye feel then?"

"Malcolm will remain here. He will ensure ye are safe. No one is going to kill ye."

She let out a huff and, once again, studied him. "Why do ye have to go?"

"Tis my duty."

Unsure what else had to be said, she decided it was best to allow him to rest. After all, it had only been a few days since they'd return from the Mackenzie's, followed by the summons by her father. Now, once again, he would be going away.

"Take Duin."

His brow furrowed. "Why would I take that beast?"

"He will be anxious to go and was a warhorse before being given to me. Duin is brave and fearless."

"I will consider it." He turned to her. "Will ye please go to sleep?"

Merida nodded. "I will, but only if ye promise me not to die."

"I will do my best not to," Tristan said and yawned. "I promise."

Feeling a bit adrift, Merida snuggled against him, her eyes stinging with unshed tears. He was her anchor there amongst the Ross Clan. Without him, she would be adrift.

"Sleep." Tristan rolled onto his back and pulled her closer. Her throat constricted when her husband pressed a kiss to the top of her head. Within minutes, a soft snore told her that he'd fallen asleep. Her mind awhirl, Merida could only stare up into the darkness while wishing days would race by so that he would once again hold her at night.

MERIDA STOOD AT the top of an incline just outside the front gates of the keep. Her right foot slightly lifted, she leaned on Elspeth for balance.

Seeing the large number of horsemen lined up and preparing to leave, she wondered how it was that her entire clan was not slaughtered when battling with them.

There were one hundred and fifty men present and that was less than half of the entire army that Malcolm Ross commanded.

"Impressive, isn't it?" Elspeth said. "At the same time, it's frightening."

Merida nodded. "It is."

Ian and Tristan stood just in front of them with Malcolm, each of them impressive in stance and stature. Tristan was taller than Malcolm by a hair and Ian just a bit shorter than the brothers.

Tristan turned to her, his gaze seeming to bore into her soul. Then he neared, pressed a kiss to her lips and walked to where Duin was being held steady by Tristan's cousin, Ruari.

The beast's head lifted and lowered and he pawed the ground, anxious to be loosed and allowed to run. Merida looked at the horse and rider and her heart tugged. She'd asked Tristan to take Duin because the beast had a quality that warriors treasured in a warhorse. He would give his life protecting the man that rode into battle with him. Duin had fought off many an attack being ridden by one of her uncles, who'd died in battle years earlier.

And although other men attempted to take the horse, he would have no one but Merida near. And now the proud beast had chosen Tristan. Merida wondered if once fighting with him, Duin would ever be hers again.

As the men rode off, Merida turned away, not wishing to see so many backs departing.

"There is much to do this morning," Elspeth said, tugging her sleeve. "I plan to help out in the garden this morning. Would ye like to come?"

Merida nodded. "I may be more of an inconvenience, but I will help where I can. It will be a good distraction."

She was loaded onto a small cart and a guardsman pulled it to where Elspeth instructed. A short fence around the far side of the main house closed in the garden. In the green space, Moira kept a well-stocked garden patch.

Upon Merida being assisted down, she hobbled to a small stool. Elspeth slid a look to her.

"I know this is a difficult adjustment for ye. Do not hesitate to come to me. I will ensure ye will never be lonely."

"Thank ye." Merida wanted to go to the bedchamber and cry, not garden and make small talk. How could Elspeth not understand this?

The vegetable garden was more than ready to be harvested. Carrots were ready to be dug up and huge cabbages needed to be plucked from the ground. Using their aprons to carry items, two maids walked between the neat rows, inspecting what needed to be harvested.

Elspeth greeted her friend, Ceilidh, who stood by the gate with a forlorn expression. Ceilidh attempted a smile at Merida, but then sniffed and wiped an errant tear.

"He did not speak to me before leaving," she said by way of explanation. Elspeth slid a look to Merida. "We thought that she and Ian would be courting by now, but he seems to not wish to. He avoids Ceilidh at all costs."

Ceilidh wiped her nose on the edge of her apron. "I am not going to mope for him. If he is going to ignore me, I will do the same from now on."

Despite feeling a bit sad herself, Merida wanted to chuckle. It would be easy to ignore a man who was gone from there. "Why do ye think he ignores ye?"

The woman gave a dainty shrug. "The loss of his arm, I suppose. However, he seemed keen to court while he was recovering. Now that he is well and able, Ian has changed."

Elspeth patted Ceilidh's shoulder. "It could be he is still not feeling worthy of ye. Whether a warrior or not, he may feel less than a man by missing a part of his body."

"I agree," Merida added. "I have seen men who were bawdy become subdued after losing an arm or a leg in battle."

She stopped speaking at noticing the servants stopped and stared at her as if just then realizing she was there.

One of the servants wiped at her brow. "Our clan lost many men. I know yers lost more." The young woman neared. "My brother was killed by a McLeod."

Merida swallowed past the sudden constriction in her throat. "I am sorry."

"Tis nay yer fault." The girl gave her a sad smile. "Tis the way of men."

"And we should stop talking about them," Elspeth said, opening the gate to the short fence meant to keep the goats out. Merida and Ceilidh, carrying the stool, followed. After grabbing baskets, they began to help with the harvest.

"What do ye suppose Moira will have us cook today?" one of the girls asked the other. They turned to Elspeth. "Have ye instructed her as of yet?"

Elspeth shook her head and chuckled. "I find it best to allow Moira liberty when it comes to the meals. Although my mother taught me to cook, tis not my finest work."

The camaraderie of the women, combined with the servant girl's earlier comment, settled Merida. Although her mind kept returning to Tristan, she did her best to concentrate on the moment.

No matter where or the circumstances, to her, it seemed women were stronger when it came to keeping the home in order. It was women who ensured that the bairns were taken care of, clothes washed and mended, and meals prepared and on the table every day.

Although men liked to think of themselves as protectors of the land, women ensured the home was secure. At the realization, Merida smiled up at the sky. Women did have a purpose and were as brave as men. Why had she not thought it before?

They worked for hours until the sun began to set. Merida was glad for the work. It took her mind away from the fact that once she went to sleep, she'd be alone for the first night of many to come.

Earlier in the afternoon, Ceilidh had gone to her village to spend time with her parents who'd arrived to visit earlier that day to fetch her.

"Ye should come inside and change for last meal," said Elsa, who'd been helping in the kitchen. Elsa had come out and watched them work.

Along with Elspeth, Merida went to a rain barrel and they took turns scooping water with a pot to rinse off the dirt from their hands, arms and faces.

"Once last meal is over, we should spend time in the upstairs sitting room. I need to catch up on mending and ye can perhaps do the same. It will help ye settle into a routine," Elspeth said, seeming quite content at having her as a companion.

"Thank ye so much." Merida wanted to cry in relief. "Ye have no idea how..."

"I know exactly how ye feel," Elspeth interrupted. "Malcolm has gone away for different reasons and being here with strangers was one of the most frightful things since marrying. I was so thankful when Ceilidh agreed to remain as my companion."

It was hard to picture the kind woman with Laird Ross. Malcolm Ross was intimidating and quite unapproachable. Although from all the accounts she'd heard since arriving, people felt he was softening somewhat, she could not see it. It was as if the man were made of stone. He rarely showed any emotion, his expression that of someone without feelings. The only time his gaze seemed to soften was when looking upon his wife. And even then, it was quickly gone.

Merida imagined that when they were alone, he was perhaps different, as her new friend seemed quite content and enamored by her husband.

"How is the younger brother? Is he as menacing as yer husband?" Merida asked and quickly attempted to change her words. "I mean, Laird Ross seems to be a rigid man."

Elspeth chuckled. "My husband is not a friendly person, I agree." Her face beamed as she looked toward the great room where the laird sat in a chair listening to the last of the clan's people who'd come with grievances or asking for assistance in certain matters.

"However," Elspeth continued, "I do see a different side of him when we are alone that no one else does. I expect tis the same between ye and Tristan. If not yet, once ye become better acquainted, it will be."

Merida decided to wait to discuss anything about her relationship until they were alone in the sitting room. "We have not spent much time together as of yet."

"True," Elspeth replied. "Now, about the youngest brother, Kieran. He is…" Elspeth broke off and sighed. "Not in the least likeable."

Merida felt her eyes round. What if he returned while Tristan was gone? Could it be that Kieran Ross was like Ethan? Without care for who he hurt.

"I will have to prepare ye for when he returns. If I thought Malcolm to be heartless at one time, I will have to say that in the few interactions I have had with Kieran, I consider him to be frightening. He is filled with rage and fury unlike any I have ever seen."

Merida shivered. "I hope he stays away then."

It was endearing when Elspeth giggled. "Tis a good wish."

CHAPTER NINETEEN

IT WAS DEFINITELY colder in the north and Tristan became more annoyed at the intruders as they arrived at the guard posts.

Once inside a walled area in front of the main building, Clan Ross warriors busied themselves setting up tents and gathering wood for bonfires, which would keep them busy until time to sleep.

His brother stood atop a watchtower, his long hair blowing in the wind. With the light golden hair, he looked more Norse than Highlander. His hazel gaze traveled across the men that came with Tristan and he raised an arm in greeting.

Tristan returned with his own acknowledgement, lifting his right hand up to his brother.

"Tis good to see ye," a warrior said as he neared. "They are only a day's ride away now."

Although he understood it could come to war, Tristan hoped that upon seeing the number of warriors prepared to defend their land, the idiots would turn around and leave. However, after traveling so far, the enemy probably had some sort of reinforcements or at least a plan of attack.

He walked into a large, fortified building that had been built almost fifty years earlier by his grandfather upon Clan Ross settling the northern border. It was a square structure with guard posts on every corner of the roof. The towers had arrow slits. On the roof were two large pits filled with wood that blazed constantly. Arrows could be lit and shot down not only piercing an individual, but also burning the flesh.

On the main floor was a large room where meals were served and there were several smaller rooms used for sleeping when men were off duty. On the second floor, there were open areas for sleeping during inclement weather. It was safer for the warriors to sleep outside and not all be caught inside the building, so the larger room was rarely used.

There was an enclosed area to the side, four tall walls keeping it safe from arrows and such where a blacksmith shop was.

Food was prepared outside, the area protected by a wood and thatch roof. Meals were prepared over an open fire by a man and two helpers.

Tristan walked into the main room just as Kieran came down the stairwell and entered. His brother frowned. "They arrive in a day."

"I've been told," Tristan replied. "Ian and fifty have gone to the northwest border. More of them are headed there."

Kieran shook his head. "Is Uncle Gregor with ye?"

It wasn't the time to tell his brother what had happened back at their home. Not now before what was to come. Instead, he decided to wait and discuss their uncle's injury and his marriage to Merida until once the battling ended.

"Nay. He remained back at home. Malcolm asked him to stay."

Kieran nodded. "He was not too happy about it, I bet."

"He was not."

Tristan followed Kieran to a large table atop which was a map. As they studied it, the cook's assistants entered with mugs of hot mulled cider.

The hot liquid warmed Tristan through as he continued to study the map. "Do ye think they will attack?" he asked his brother.

Kieran considered the question. "Unless they travel east and then approach, they will not have the vantage point to see how many men await here. They are about fifty or sixty in number." His brother pointed to a place on the map. "I have archers there in wait. They will send a scout back with news once the aggressors arrive. It will give us time to set up."

"Perhaps we should consider allowing them to see our men. It may discourage them from attacking."

A man entered. His name was Naill and he was a head archer, a position equal to Kieran. Naill had traveled there with Tristan.

The two archers had never gotten along. Although amusing at times, he hoped they'd not argue this day.

"Where should we go and wait?" The man peered down at the map, ignoring Kieran.

Tristan waited for Kieran to instruct the archer and once the man departed, he searched out a bed to claim, deciding it was best to get as much rest as possible before the announcement of the approaching enemy.

⋙⋘

JUST AFTER DAWN, the scout, on horseback, galloped into the camp announcing the northern warriors had traveled most of the night, arriving earlier than expected. Ross warriors scrambled to dress, grabbed their shields and swords and hurried to prepare their horses.

Within an hour, every single warrior was mounted and headed to an open field atop a hill where they had the advantage of visibility. From where they formed, land was visible for miles.

Archers on horseback lined up side-by-side a distance forward from everyone else. With the advantage of sight and height, this would be a battle led by bows and arrows.

Kieran, atop his horse, was in line with the archers at the front. Once the archers began the assault, if the approaching fighters got past a point they'd predetermined, then the other Ross warriors would rush into the battle.

The thundering of horses' hooves vibrated the ground and Duin shifted side to side, his giant feet pawing at the ground. The beast was as anxious as Tristan to ride into battle. His own heartbeat accelerated and his breathing deepened as he kept his eyes on the horizon.

Moments later, the front lines of the northern fighters came into view, the men slowing at spotting Clan Ross.

"There are fewer than I thought," Tristan said to the fighter next to him. "Perhaps forty."

"Aye," the man said, eyes narrowed.

"Ready!" Kieran called out and the archers lifted their bows, arrows set to fly high before descending.

There was a standoff as the northern fighters seemed to regroup. Like the Ross' warriors, they, too, had archers, but the warriors moved around to the front so that their archers would defend from behind.

The intruding warriors lifted their shields.

"They mean to fight," Tristan mumbled. "Fools."

"Sans Peur! Sans Peur!" With primal yells, the northern men rushed forward.

Clan Sutherland.

Although they'd not had an unfriendly relationship with the northern clan, they'd been aware of the new laird's desire to grow his territory.

"Loose!" Kieran yelled and arrows flew into the air. About ten Sutherland men fell, but it didn't slow the momentum of other warriors rushing forward.

Duin began to prance and Tristan knew the feeling. It was hard to allow archers to fight for them but, at the moment, it seemed to be working better than hand-to-hand combat, when another dozen fell from horses.

The few that were left rode sideways but continued forward in zigzag patterns that would be a good defense in a wooded area, but not in the open field. Another five or so were felled quickly.

Shouts sounded from the back of the lines and the men that were left turned around and galloped back to where they had come from. Only a couple tried to save those on the ground.

"Loose!" Kieran yelled again and more arrows flew. A couple men fell when pierced in the back, some continued riding with arrows protruding from their bodies.

Tristan lifted an arm and commanded his warriors to give chase. They would not fight this day, but a clear message was sent to Laird Sutherland. He'd just made a formidable enemy.

There were many survivors, as arrows didn't always kill. Tristan and other warriors walked amongst the injured. He hoisted a man up who had an arrow piercing through his stomach. The man swayed, his eyes unfocused.

"Horse!" Tristan called. Another warrior brought a horse forward. Together, they hoisted the injured man onto the horse. "Tell yer laird that next time there will be no survivors." He wrapped the animal's reins around the man's wrists and hit the horse on the rump.

Several more survivors were helped onto horses and the same message was given. One man in particular met Tristan's gaze as he broke the arrow that protruded from his leg. Another had pierced his left arm and Tristan pushed it through. After that, he took the man's belt and tied it around the upper arm. "Thank ye. I have a wife and three bairns to return to."

"Yer laird should have considered our size before sending ye to fight."

The man nodded and headed away.

Only a handful of men lay dead on the ground. Tristan did not take time to look at them. Instead, he went to find Duin as he wished to go back to the camp. Considering the lack of fighting, he wondered if the conversation with his brother would be harder.

There was no way to gauge what Kieran's reaction would be to finding out about his marriage, the attack when returning from the Mackenzie's and their uncle's injury. Then there was the matter of the continued truce with the McLeods.

Later that day, a simple meal of mutton and bread was served as everyone settled for the evening.

Tristan and the warriors would wait another week before returning, as they wanted to ensure the Sutherland did not attack again.

Seated at a small table with Kieran and Naill, Tristan dipped his bread into the broth and plopped it into his mouth.

"I heard that Duncan Sutherland had taken over for his father who is on his death bed," Kieran said between bites of bread. "He's trying to make his mark."

Tristan agreed. "Which is why we cannot be certain of what he will do next. A new and young power-hungry man is dangerous."

"True," Kieran replied. "How is Malcolm?"

The question took Tristan by surprise. "He carries the yoke of laird well. Works all day with the clan's people. I think they are testing him, and finding he is harsher than father was."

Kieran seemed to mull over what Tristan had said. "He is a good man."

"Ye are as well, Brother."

"Why do ye say that?" Kieran snapped. "I do not care to be a good person. I care for nothing."

"Ye care for me and our family."

"Do not be fooled." Kieran stood and stalked out from the room.

Naill huffed. "He is like a rabid boar lately."

"He is still Kieran. Time will help."

Although Tristan felt a duty to defend his brother, at the same time he wondered if his brother would soften over time. Sullen and withdrawn since he was a young man, a series of events had changed him forever. The dying of their father in his presence had only made it worse. Perhaps Kieran cared for no one. In truth, he would not be surprised if it was so.

TWO DAYS LATER, there were no signs of the other clan returning. Tristan rode Duin to the edge of the field where the battle had been. The bodies of the dead were gone and he assumed Sutherland men had come during the night and retrieved them.

In the distance, Kieran appeared. Riding a black warhorse, his younger brother returned from checking on the archers who remained on post. Even from the distance, Kieran was impressive. Large and muscular, he didn't look like most of the archers who, for the most part, were lithe. His brother was an expert marksman with the bow and arrow, but also impressive with a sword. When Kieran neared and met his gaze, the ever-present scowl on his face, Tristan noted a deep scratch across his cheek.

"What happened to yer face?"

"Branch," Kieran replied, wiping blood away with his arm.

Tristan inspected the wound. "Ye sure it was not from an irate lass? Perhaps someone finally bested the champion?"

His brother did not jest, ever. Instead, his scowl deepened. Interesting that of the three, Kieran was the most striking and also, perhaps, the most feared.

His features often took people by surprise. Perfect is what he was often described as. With a regal nose, long-lashed, light hazel eyes and lips that women desired, it was hard for most not to take note. Of course, being he was never of good temper, most people did their best to avoid him.

"Can we talk?" Tristan said, dismounting. "Tis important."

He decided it was best to approach Kieran when they were out and away from the others.

Kieran dismounted and loosed his horse to graze. Tristan didn't trust Duin to do the same, so he held the animal's reins. Then when noting the animal seemed relaxed enough, he dropped them.

"I have never seen that horse before," Kieran said, studying Duin. "Where did ye get him?"

Tristan took a breath. "He belongs to my wife."

"Wife?" Kieran narrowed his eyes. "What happened?"

"The Mackenzie beckoned Malcolm to a meeting. I went in his stead. While I was there, the Mackenzie demanded I marry a woman of his choosing. In an effort to keep his territory safe, he made many demands of our clan. Most were refused.

"A Munro?" Kieran asked and Tristan wondered if it was Kieran's way of hoping what he dreaded was not true.

"Nay. A McLeod."

Kieran inhaled sharply and he glared at Tristan, his mouth twisting into a snarl. "Why would ye agree?"

"Both me and the McLeod did not agree to it. I did my best to dissuade the Mackenzie and when he would not bend, I put him off. I waited for Uncle Gregor to come and arbitrate a different outcome. However, the Mackenzie would not change his mind."

Still as a statue, the only thing that moved were Kieran's lips as they formed a tight line. "Peace will never be achieved as long as Ethan McLeod lives."

"They are aware we will never cease to hunt him."

"What else?" Kieran knew him enough to sense Tristan was holding something back. Already surprised at the fact his brother was somewhat rational, he wondered if he should tell the man everything.

"I married Merida McLeod. Malcolm and I met with the McLeod after returning home. We demanded Ethan's head, but he refused. The McLeod said that he was confined."

"Ye believe him?"

"No."

Tristan paused. "Kieran," Tristan began and stopped at the dangerous gleam in his brother's eyes. "There is more."

Silence stretched, so Tristan began to speak. "I left the Mackenzie keep without waiting for word to be sent to either clan about the marriage. I was angry and did not wish to remain and give the Mackenzie time to come up with other demands. We were attacked. Uncle Gregor was injured."

Kieran's eyes bored into Tristan's, but he did not speak.

"He is recovering, but one of our men died."

"McLeods?"

"Aye."

"Is there anything else, Brother?" Kieran spoke between clenched teeth.

"Other than a temporary truce with the McLeods, no. That is all."

Kieran went to his horse, mounted and looked down to Tristan. "I do not know how ye and Malcolm could stand to be near even one of them. The McLeods killed our father and now ye bring one into our home? I will not live with a McLeod. She must leave."

"We are married. I made a vow…"

"No one would have been the wiser if ye had killed her during the attack. The McLeods would have been blamed."

His brother rode off. Tristan cursed and raked both hands down his face. Hopefully, Kieran would calm before returning to the keep. He turned to look for Duin, but the cursed horse had gone.

"Argh!"

CHAPTER TWENTY

MERIDA TOOK A tentative step, glad that her ankle did not ache as much as before. Although she didn't want to overdo it, she hated depending on anyone to help her about. Certainly, the guard who helped her didn't seem to mind, but she'd caught him looking down her bodice already more than once.

Elsa, her companion, entered, her eyes wide. "Two women have arrived. They seem very cross and agitated."

"Who are they?" Merida asked.

"I do not recognize them." Not that either of them would recognize anyone there. Elsa went to the bed and began smoothing the bedding.

"I will not remain here cowering." When she stepped out of the chamber Merida shared with Tristan, the corridor was empty.

A plan in mind, she walked toward the stairwell. After a quick, simple meal, she'd decided to spend the morning with Elspeth. They planned an outing to the village, which she was both a bit scared of and excited for at the same time.

Elspeth assured her the villagers wouldn't be hostile toward her. "They are much more interested in the fact that we have a truce than who one of the laird's family marries."

Hopefully, it was true.

"I will not stand for it." At an unfamiliar woman's loud statement, Merida stopped in her tracks, halfway down the stairs.

Two women with matching scowls glared at Malcolm. Next to him, Elspeth seemed at a loss, hands clutched together.

The older woman of the two held up both hands, fingers like talons. "She must be sent away immediately. Neither Verity nor I will remain in this house with a woman from that clan. They killed yer father, have ye forgotten it so soon?"

Lady Ross.

Merida had hoped Tristan's mother and sister would not return until after he did. There was no one to protect her now. Elspeth was barely tolerated by the woman, so she expected worse.

Malcolm had never exchanged a word with her since she'd arrived. Now, she stood with her back against the wall, waiting to hear what they would decide to do.

Already in her mind, she inventoried her belongings and decided that she and Elsa could leave immediately. Given a small cart, a horse could pull them and the few items she owned without problem.

"Mother, please sit. Ye must be tired after yer travels." Malcolm took the woman's elbow. He motioned to a nearby servant. "Bring warmed cider."

Lady Ross allowed him to guide her to a chair, her expression not changing. "Tell me why ye allowed this to happen?"

Verity must have sensed her presence because she turned and looked to Merida, her expression thunderous. "Why are ye spying on us?"

"Go away," Lady Ross exclaimed, following her daughter's line of vision. "Far away."

She was not about to be treated as an inferior. Merida hitched her chin. A laird's daughter did not coward.

At Malcolm's nod, Elspeth went to Merida. "Come, let us break our fast in the kitchen."

They made their way to the back of the room, all the while sensing the two women's glares.

"She is Tristan's wife and will remain. Both of ye will accept it or ye are welcome to move to the smaller house." Malcolm's response made Merida stumble forward. Had Laird Ross just stood up for her?

"How can ye do this?" Lady Ross shrieked and jumped to her feet. "I will not stand for this."

"Tis yer choice."

Elspeth slowed upon noticing that Merida was having trouble keeping up. They were in the corridor just outside the kitchens.

Face flushed, Elspeth looked around to ensure they were alone. "She acted the same way when I came here."

"I should leave," Merida said. "I will never be fully accepted by the family. Imagine what it will be like when Kieran returns."

"No doubt, Tristan is preparing him. He did plan to inform his brother of what happened since he left did he not?" Elspeth patted her on the arm.

"In truth, we did not speak of it. We spoke of little, barely had any time." Merida sighed suddenly, wishing Tristan were there. Not for the first time, she yearned for her husband. As foreign as it was, she'd come to think of him as her partner.

They moved aside to allow a servant to scurry by with a tray of aromatic spiced cider.

"Let us go eat," Elspeth said. "This will all sort itself out."

Merida wasn't sure it ever would. But she walked alongside Elspeth to the kitchens.

Later that day, Merida and Elspeth remained in the sitting room. It was best to avoid the Ross women and not cause any further conflict. Merida looked to the doorway upon hearing footsteps and held her breath.

"Why are ye in here?" Verity froze at the entryway and glared at

Merida. "This is my sitting room."

Elspeth sighed. "Why are ye so disagreeable? As the laird's wife, I have the final say when it comes to this home. Merida and I will sit wherever we wish."

The young woman had a round face and small mouth. The only resemblance to her brothers was the color of her eyes. Unfortunately, they were small and unremarkable. Merida wondered why the males in the family seemed to have been graced with the more agreeable features.

Verity straightened and hitched her chin. "My brother will hear about this immediately."

"Malcolm is busy with much more important matters. If ye wish to sit in here alone, we will leave and go to the garden." She looked to Merida. "It is much too beautiful a day to remain indoors in the gloom anyway."

They lifted their sewing baskets and walked out.

Merida hesitated. "Would ye like to join us, Verity? Perhaps if we get to know each other, ye will think differently of me."

The woman's mouth fell open and her small eyes widened. "I most certainly would not."

She wasn't sure, but she thought she heard Elspeth giggle.

"Lady Ross is worse," Elspeth whispered. "I do not know how they can remain so disagreeable about everything."

The women had reason to hate her. Her brother had killed their husband and father. Followed by the war between the clans, there was a lot of resentment. It did not excuse the women's behavior, but she did not begrudge them either. She supposed if a Ross had killed her father, she'd not wish to have a member of their family in her home either.

As far as Elspeth went, Lady Ross probably expected that as laird, her son would marry a woman of higher standing.

"Once Tristan returns, perhaps it would be best if he and I move to the smaller home and not displace Lady Ross or Verity."

They stepped outside. The day was, indeed, pleasant. The sun was shining and only a few clouds hovered in the sky. A pang of homesickness unsettled Merida and she blinked away tears. She and her mother always went for walks on days like these.

"Would ye mind that we walk instead of sitting?" Merida asked Elspeth. "I tire of sitting about."

Elspeth gave her an impish grin. "I agree. I miss my long walks in the forest."

They walked around to the back of the keep. From there, they moved through a gate. Elspeth looked up to the roof and waved. A guard looked down then motioned another set of men, who also peered down. An archer gave Elspeth a sign to go ahead and the pair of women made their way down a small hill to an open field.

"This is lovely," Merida exclaimed at seeing a blanket of purplish flowers. "Why have we not come out here?"

Elspeth sighed. "So much has been happening lately, it was only a few days ago that Malcolm allowed me to leave the security of the walls." She motioned up to the roof where the men continued to peer down. "I have to ensure they are aware I am out here so we will be constantly watched."

"I don't mind at all," Merida said, turning in a full circle, her arms out. "The flowers smell delightful."

They meandered for a while, seeking out the different types of flowers and deciding which to pick to use and decorate the great room. Upon spotting a doe with a couple of young fawns, they crouched down and watched the animals until they disappeared into the trees.

"Are the guards not afraid someone will come from the forest and attack?"

"Nay," Elspeth replied, looking to the trees. "These are Ross hunting grounds. Our guards are always out there in the forest either hunting for the day's meal or ensuring there are no trespassers."

Merida's father had an area that was designated for him as well. He was quite stern about anyone else coming onto that portion of his land. Usually a calm man, he lost his temper when a trespasser was brought before him. The trespasser was given a fine and made to remain locked in a cage in the center of the courtyard for three days with only bread and water.

It was a light sentence but most found it embarrassing enough to deter them from repeating the offense.

"When Tristan returns, ye should come out here and spend time together, talking and getting to know one another," Elspeth counseled. "It is hard enough to be somewhere where ye feel uncared for without at least having yer husband's support."

Merida nodded, her eyes misting. "I had a friend who I visited often. He lives in a cottage in the woods not far from my keep. I wonder what he is thinking, if he has tried to find me."

"Is he yer love?" Elspeth peered at her with interest. "What will ye do?"

"No, Grier is a monk. A healer. He taught me a great deal about..."

"A monk?" Elspeth said in a high tone. "Does he have a mole right here?" She pressed a finger to the left side of her face just below her nose."

"Aye, he does." Merida's mouth fell open. "Have ye met Grier?"

"I think so." Elspeth lifted both hands to her cheeks. "Can it be? I have often wondered what happened to him. Ye see, he taught me all I know about herbs and such. But I always called him 'Teacher'. It was strange that I never asked his name."

"We must go find him," Merida said with a smile. "Perhaps there is a way to get a message to him to meet us."

Elspeth thought about it. "We should."

⋙⋘

AS CLAN'S PEOPLE trickled in from the villages, the weight of responsibilities pressed down on Malcolm's shoulders. His mother and sister remained sitting at the table with him. They took turns demanding he remove Merida with the same arguments over and over. As much as he hated disappointing them, it was best to not make a decision without Tristan present.

Verity would be gone soon to marry a son of the Munro laird. The wedding had already been postponed twice due to conflicts and winter. However, now that they'd returned from visiting, it would finally occur.

"Perhaps I will go live with Verity, since my own son turns his back on me," his mother sniffed. "Yer father would be so disappointed."

Not wishing the people arriving to hear, Malcolm stood. "We will continue to discuss this tonight. I must see to my duties. Please go to yer chambers and rest."

Hoping they'd do as he asked, Malcolm went to the high board and was joined by two of the clan's advisors. Thankfully, there were not too many people there that day.

A farmer came forward first to claim his herd of goats had been dwindling since the truce. He blamed McLeods, but given that his farm was in the southern portion of the lands, that was doubtful.

"Warriors arrive," a guard announced later that day. "Our warriors."

Malcolm hurried out and up the stairs over the gates. In the distance, he saw that about fifty men rode toward the keep. The battle, if there was one, was obviously in their favor and they didn't bring any injured back with them.

The head archer, Naill, raced toward the keep and Malcolm hurried down to the courtyard.

"Aye, Laird," Naill called out dismounting. The man grinned. "Twas a battle fought only by archers."

"Ours and theirs?

"Mostly ours." The large man came forward, a huge bow and filled quiver strapped to his wide back. "With less than half our number, it didn't take long for them to realize they had no chance of winning."

"Any Ross injuries?"

"Nay. Unless ye count a cut finger." Naill held up his hand, showing a bandaged thumb. "Too quick on my drawing of arrows."

"That is unlike ye," Malcolm replied in a light tone. He'd not become comfortable enough to allow his walls down around the warriors, preferring to keep a part of him sealed away. Men like Naill were not guaranteed to be alive longer than the next battle. Malcolm didn't relish the idea of becoming close to someone only for them to die.

Himself included. As laird, there were always people who wished him dead.

"Who were they?"

"Sutherlands."

"Why would the Sutherland attack?"

"His son has taken the role of laird," Naill replied.

It made sense. The younger Sutherland was a weakling who tried to prove himself in the wrong way. "My brothers?"

"They are well. Tristan returns in a few days."

"Kieran?"

Naill shrugged. Aware of the animosity between Naill and Kieran, Malcolm didn't ask more.

"I'm off to see my wife," Naill said, grabbing himself between the legs.

Malcolm gave him a flat look. "I will speak to the men." Stable lads had neared with his horse and he mounted. Once within hearing distance of the men who'd remained mounted and in lines, he held up a hand to get their attentions.

"Ye have proven yer loyalty to our clan and its people. I offer my gratitude. It will be known that we are not a weak clan and our borders are strong."

The warriors cheered and began dispersing. Some of the men went to the villages where they lived and the bachelors continued into the keep to their quarters.

CHAPTER TWENTY-ONE

A week later.

THE GATES OPENED and upon entering the keep courtyard, Tristan could only think of finding Merida. She was not outdoors that he could see, neither for that matter was any member of his family. He'd thought that upon it being announced that he had arrived, someone would come out to greet him.

Not thinking much about it, he guided Duin to the stables, where lads met him and attempted to take the horse. Immediately, Duin reared up on two legs, his giant front hooves in the air.

The lads scrambled back in fear.

"I will take him to the stable," Tristan grumbled and continued as he guided the unmanageable beast away. "Something has to be done about ye, horse. Ye must learn to allow someone other than me and Merida…"

Ruari chuckled. "Talking to yerself, Cousin?"

"This horse will not allow anyone near it. Tis only Merida and me that he doesn't attempt to kill."

"Let me see." Ruari neared, his hand out, palm down. He ran his hand down the animal's nose. "Quite contrary, are ye?" he asked the horse in a soft voice. "Come along now or else ye will not be fed." His cousin lifted a wooden bucket of oats. "There may be a carrot in here."

Duin's nostrils flared and he sniffed the bucket.

When Ruari led the horse away, Tristan shook his head. Perhaps there was hope for the unruly animal.

At a rain barrel, Tristan took a pot that hung from a rope next to it. He dipped the wooden bowl into the water and poured it over his head and neck. Next, he washed his lower arms and hands. More than anything, he wanted to go for a swim. But at the moment, it was best to speak to Malcolm and see what had happened in the household while he was away.

There was the matter of Kieran, who'd not spoken to him again about his marriage. Neither did his younger brother reply to Tristan's questions of whether or not he'd remain away from the McLeods for now.

Chickens scrambled out of the way as he made his way to the entrance. Once he was inside the entryway, he hesitated to allow his eyes to adjust to the dimness of the interior.

Although his father had ordered large windows on both sides of the great room, it was still a bit dim compared to outdoors.

Malcolm held court, two farmers arguing before him. Another set of villagers' voices rose while in a rather heated discussion about whatever they came to see his brother about.

At a table, a woman held a screaming child while her husband stood by, pretending not to hear.

Two young men were tugging at a rope that was tied to a goat, each attempting to take ownership. Meanwhile, a young village girl stood between her parents, crying and seeming to plead about something. By the looks of a terrified young man who stood by her burly father, he was the cause of whatever consternation was at hand.

At once, Tristan understood why no one had come outside to greet him. In one corner of the room, Elspeth and Merida were tending to a man who bled from his forehead. The entire time, the man pointed and cussed at another who stood by with a snarl and fists on his hips.

His mother and Verity were also present. They took turns glaring at him, as they seemed to be waiting to speak to Malcolm who was doing his best to ignore them.

Tristan walked down the center of the room, held both hands up and shouted, "Shut up!"

Everyone, including the wailing baby, went silent.

"Now, that's better." He pointed at the boys with the goat. "Come here."

The boys neared and the closer they got, the more timid they became. It was almost comical when both dropped the rope. Tristan crossed his arms, knowing it would make his muscles bunch. "Whose goat is it?"

"Mine," the freckle-faced boy of the duo said. "He gave it to me."

Tristan looked to the other and frowned. "Did ye?"

"Aye, but he doesn't care for it properly. Tis skinny now." The boy pointed at the goat, which in Tristan's estimation looked to be in good shape. "Ye can see its ribs. Look."

"I feed him daily, sir," the freckle-faced boy said. The goat ambled away as if without a care in the world.

Tristan pointed at the freckle-faced boy. "See that he's fed properly." He then looked to the other. "If he doesn't, come back and tell me."

The boys nodded and rushed off. The freckle-faced one tugged the goat away from a table. The animal grabbed a chunk of bread and swallowed it.

Ignoring his mother stalking toward him, Tristan went next to the parents, the crying girl and the frightened boy. "What is happening here?"

It was hours later that the room finally emptied. Only a few people, who lived too far to return home before dark, remained. They would partake in last meal and spend the night there.

"Ye came back just in time," Malcolm said, sitting back. His brother blew out a breath and eyed his tankard. But he seemed to decide it took too much energy to actually drink it. "How did Da do this for so many years?"

"Not all days are like this."

"Aye, true."

Malcolm chuckled. "Did ye really order that boy to marry the crying girl?"

"Aye," Tristan laughed. "Neither her father nor the lad wished it, but it was obvious the girl is with bairn."

"Ah."

Their mother rose and stalked over. "Will ye make time for yer mother now?"

"What is it, Mother?" Malcolm said in a patient voice.

"That woman. She cannot be out and about as if she belongs here."

Tristan was aware that she spoke of Merida. He looked about the room. He'd been so busy with everything, he'd yet to greet her. "My wife…"

"She can do as she wishes. I have told ye this, Mother," Malcolm interrupted.

That his brother had stood up for Merida in his absence touched him and Tristan had to swallow past the lump forming in his throat. No matter how unyielding his brother had always been, there seemed to be a soft spot in his heart since marrying Elspeth.

"Then Verity and I will leave."

"Where will ye go, Mother?" Tristan asked. "This is yer home."

"I offered them the smaller house here in the keep," Malcolm said. "They can remain under our protection. Once Verity marries, Mother can decide to remain or go with her to the Munro keep."

Their mother placed both hands to her chest. "If yer father was here, he would never allow me to be displaced."

"Ye are correct, Mother," Tristan admitted. "Merida and I will go live in the smaller house. That way, we will not have to worry about ye and Verity feeling at odds with us."

Lady Ross' eyebrows lifted in surprise. "Ye would leave yer own home for that woman?"

"Mother," Malcolm started, but Tristan interrupted.

"She is my wife. I vowed to stand by her." In that moment, he became aware he did not plan to let his wife leave. Ever. Malcolm must have realized it, too, because he gave Tristan a knowing look.

"It seems fair to me." Malcolm let out a breath. "Mother, he remains within the keep. Our home."

Without any other thing to argue about, their mother looked to one and then the other. "Where is Kieran?"

"He remains at the northern border. He should return in a fortnight if not sooner," Tristan said.

She huffed. "He knows about her?"

"Aye." Tristan ensured to keep a neutral tone. "He is aware."

When she turned away, Verity glared at Tristan. "If Mother falls ill, it will be yer fault."

"I must see about Merida and tell her we are moving."

"Ye know Mother will leave with Verity. She will marry in but a few weeks," Malcolm added.

"Aye, but it is best to keep the peace for now."

Malcolm looked around the room and seeming to deem it safe, he spoke. "Why do ye think the Sutherland attacked?"

"The son has taken over as laird. The idiot is trying to prove himself."

"That is what I supposed. Will he try again?"

Tristan shook his head. "I do not think he will. Not for a long time. Especially after trespassing through Munro lands. A messenger was sent to the Munro asking that he, too, send a message to the Sutherland that they are not allowed to trespass."

"Good use of our new marriage alignment," Malcolm said. "What of Kieran?"

"He remains the same. I fear he may attack any McLeod he runs across and our truce will end."

Malcolm's gaze moved over the room to the windows. "The truce will not end. Kieran will not settle until he gets his revenge. In a way, I understand him. Fury remains within me as well."

AS HARD AS she tried, Merida could not help the tightening in her chest. Tristan had returned hours earlier and had yet to greet her. A part of her wondered if it was because his mother had returned.

She dipped a cloth into a basin and washed dried blood from one of Gregor Ross' wounds. He was a kind man, who she remembered from the times he'd come to meet with her father. Both he and the late laird had often hunted with her father when she was young.

The water was becoming bloody and she decided to pour it out and get more.

"Ye are recovering well," she told the older man. He did look much better.

"I am considering not traveling any more. Both times lately, I was attacked by yer clan." Although he didn't sound cross, she wasn't sure if he was or not.

"Was the other time when Tristan was injured?"

"Aye," he replied. "That time, it was my son's fault. He is a traitor."

"Where is he?"

Gregor shrugged. "Probably hiding away, never returning as he will be jailed or worse."

Wrapping his midsection, Merida helped the man settle into a chair. Although he was well enough to leave his chambers, he seemed to prefer to remain there. She didn't blame him. There was a wide balcony that overlooked the flower fields where she and Elspeth had gone just the day before. It was a beautiful day, the sun's rays bathing the area with warmth.

"Ye have the most perfect chamber, I think."

Gregor chuckled. "Do not tell anyone," he replied in a mirth-filled whisper.

"I will keep it to myself," Merida said with a smile. "Ye are very important to my husband. He was very worried about ye."

"He is special to me as well." The man looked around as if to make sure no one overheard. "He is my favorite nephew."

Merida neared and sat opposite Gregor. "I hope to get to know him better. He seems to be a kind and fair man."

"He is," Gregor replied with a nod. "An honorable young man. Ye could not wish for a better husband. I sense he has done well for a wife as well."

Her breath hitched. "Thank ye for saying that."

She looked at Gregor for a moment before continuing. "And yet, I told Tristan I wished to return to my clan. It would be for the best. Ye understand that it is very possible our clans will always be at war."

The man met her gaze with assurance. "What I know is that our clans had a strong alliance until the rash actions of yer brother. Time will heal the divide between the clans. Yer marriage will help it happen."

"Then I should remain? What about my brother?"

"That is yer decision. I do believe ye know that yer brother will meet his end, if not by one of my nephew's hands, then by another person he wrongs."

Merida nodded.

"I see ye fare better, Uncle." Tristan stood in the doorway and Merida whirled toward him, her heart pitching at the sight of the huge warrior filling the doorway.

CHAPTER TWENTY-TWO

"I WILL CARRY that." Tristan took the large bowl of bloody water from her arms. "Ye should not be carrying it, but order a servant to assist ye."

She didn't look at him. "I do what I can to keep busy."

"What of yer ankle?" He met her gaze and quickly looked away as the water sloshed, coming close to over spilling.

"It is much better." In truth, it was a bit painful, as she'd overdone it twice already. First with the walk outdoors and now carrying water back and forth.

When they came to a doorway at the end of the corridor, Merida opened it so Tristan could toss the water outdoors. He put the bowl down. When his gaze met hers, it was as if he had so much to say. But instead, he pulled her close, his mouth instantly covering hers.

The feel of his hard body against hers filled Merida with need. She clung to him as his mouth moved across her, a combination of caresses and demand. Merida lifted her arms and wrapped them around his neck, enjoying the feel of her breasts pressed against the rough fabric of his tunic.

"I need ye, Wife," Tristan mumbled against her ear. Immediately, her body reacted, heat pooling in the most uncomfortable way for one outdoors.

"Come." He pulled her further out from the doorway and held her against the exterior wall.

Cupping her bottom, Tristan lifted her so their sexes were aligned. Her skirts lifted up to her thighs when she wrapped her legs around his midsection. Already too impassioned, she couldn't care less if an entire army happened upon them.

Tristan's fast breaths blew past her ear as he held her in place, his body moving in a most pleasurable way.

"I cannot keep from taking ye right here," he said, moving a hand between them and freeing himself from the confines of his breeches.

"Yes," Merida said, barely able to catch her breath, only to gasp when his rod pressed against her entrance.

"Relax for me beauty," Tristan instructed, working his hardness up and down her core in an effort to arouse her more.

Merida took his mouth with hers, raking her fingers through his hair, needing to be closer to have more of him. When he entered her, the intrusion sent a pulse of heat up her torso, forming a cry from deep in her throat.

She bit into the fabric of his tunic in an effort to keep quiet. He slid out and thrust back into her over and over, the entire time keeping one hand on the small of her back to keep the rock wall from hurting her.

Wonderful sensations traveled through every inch of her body and yet she wanted more. As he continued the now frantic movements, Merida fought to remain coherent while at the same time barely able to keep a straight thought.

He was so powerful, so strong, each movement emphasizing his strength. Every muscle on his body bunched and loosened.

"Oh. Oh." Merida repeated as her hold on reality evaporated. Tristan continued the steady thrusts, seeming to gain more energy with each passing moment.

Finally, Merida could not stop from losing all control, her body going rigid in its release, her sex constricting around his. The sensations of her reaction affected Tristan because he let out a hoarse groan and shuddered.

Merida continued to cling to him, unable to trust that she could stand unaided. "I don't think I can walk."

"It would be noticeable if we went inside like this," he replied with a light chuckle.

"I cannot believe we are outside in broad daylight. We cannot be seen like this."

Once again, he covered her mouth with his while separating their bodies in the sweetest of ways.

He helped her to stand, but they did not move apart. Tristan pulled her against him, kissing the top of her head.

For an inexplicable reason, Merida's eyes filled with tears. Perhaps it was because he was such a comforting presence in her new life. Tristan was one person she felt fully at ease with. It was strange, as they'd not known each other long. Perhaps it was the vows, or the intimacy that made things so.

"Are ye crying?" Tristan lifted her chin and peered at her. "Did I hurt ye?"

"No, tis not that." She sniffed. "Ye did not greet me upon arriving." Now, she felt like a ninny for bringing up something so superficial. After all she had witnessed, how he'd helped his brother bring order to an otherwise chaotic situation, she decided that she was being foolish.

Merida scrambled to take back her words. "Ignore me. It is silly to bring that up. Ye had more important matters at hand."

When he kissed her again, his tongue slipped between her lips and she fell against him, enjoying the tenderness of the moment. His mouth traveled to her jawline where he continued to press kisses until reaching her ear.

Then he straightened and ensured she met his gaze. "Nothing

should be more important than greeting ye upon my return from battle. Forgive me."

Merida was astonished at his apology. The more she got to know Tristan Ross, the more fortunate she felt about being forced to marry him.

He guided her back inside and through the great room. "We must speak," he said, ignoring his mother and sister who glared at Merida. She looked up at him, wondering if perhaps something had happened, but decided to wait until they were alone to ask.

Once inside their bedchamber, he went to a truck and pulled out a clean tunic and breeches. "I am going to swim. Would ye like to come with me?"

"I am not sure," Merida replied. "The water must still be very cold."

"Aye, but I do not have patience to wait for water to be brought and heated. This way it will be faster." Grabbing a knapsack, he put the clothes in there along with a cloth from the water basin and a bar of soap.

"I would like to come with ye."

"Very well."

He seemed relaxed and of good humor, so Merida decided to ask him questions. "Did ye talk with yer mother about me?"

"Aye. She and Verity wanted to move to the smaller house. I offered that ye and I would move instead." He stopped from inspecting a tartan and turned to her. "Do ye agree?"

"I prefer it, actually," she said, meaning it while at the same time shocked that he'd asked her opinion. "It will be more comfortable for all of us."

"I cannot promise Mother will come around to ever accepting ye. Too much has happened."

Merida sighed. "Aye, I understand. Perhaps one day, she will understand that I did not have anything to do with yer father's death."

"We all know that, Merida." It was the first time she'd heard him say her name and she smiled at him. "Tis the first time ye have said my name."

A frown formed. "I do not believe so."

"It is."

He came to her and pulled her to him, his large arms surrounding and protecting Merida. "I will do my best to protect ye, Merida, and keep ye safe. I know ye will be a bit lonely but, after a time, I am sure things will get better."

"I have Elsa. Also Elspeth and Ceilidh are most wonderful to me."

For one of the first times since meeting him, he smiled. The action brought crinkles to the corners of his eyes and she thought it made him even more handsome. "I am glad to hear it."

Moments later, they walked side by side to the loch. Several guards came along and others were already there. It had not occurred to Merida that the other men would also want to bathe after the long trek from the northern border.

"Mayhap I should return." Merida looked around to see if there were any other women there. Just a short distance away, three women stood huddled together, their loud snickers making the men scowl in their directions.

"I could go stand with them," she offered.

"Nay," Tristan said, frowning in the direction of the women. "Those women are not the decent sort."

It was then that she noticed one of the men walking toward the women, taking one by the hand and leading her away.

"Oh," Merida said, looking away.

Tristan placed a hand on the small of her back and guided her to the water's edge, but away from the others. "Sit there and watch my things," he said and began to undress.

First, he removed his boots and then his breeches, leaving his long legs exposed. They were muscular and well-formed from riding. Next, he yanked the tunic up and over his head, handing it to her. Merida could only watch transfixed by her astonishingly muscle-ridden husband. He dove into the water and she remained still, unsure if normal breathing would ever be possible again.

In the distance, the deep murmurs of men bathing and swimming filled the air. The breeze blew over the treetops and she looked up to see that the sun was falling. Soon it would be last meal. Hopefully, Lady Ross would not make it too unbearable.

With Tristan by her side, she would feel safe despite any situation. At the thought of them living in the smaller house, she was glad for it. Even after Lady Ross and Verity moved away, she would probably prefer to stay there. It would make life much easier and she and Tristan would have the added privacy away from the people who came seeking their laird.

When Tristan came out of the water, he was shivering. She held up the cloth and rubbed the rough fabric over his body to help warm him.

As they returned toward the keep, Merida noticed that most of the men paid her little heed. Perhaps it was their respect for Tristan, but she hoped it was the first step toward them accepting her.

She peered up at her husband, noting how his hair curled at the nape of his head. He seemed to prefer it cropped, but she liked it a bit longer like it was now. "I would like to discuss something with ye," she started. "About yer brother."

"Which one?" He slid a glance to her. "Malcolm or Kieran?"

"Kieran."

He exhaled. "Ye're worried about him?"

"Aye. I hear he is dangerous. Did ye tell him about me? Us?"

"I did. And his reaction was as I expected. My brother is filled with rage. He was there when Da was killed by yer brother, ye see."

It was hard to imagine how horrible it must have been for the man. She shook her head. "I did not know. It is understandable why he is so angry then."

Tristan stopped and turned to her. "I cannot promise ye that Kieran will ever be kind to ye. He will not harm ye as he has never been violent toward women. Kieran may be a lot of things, but he does not abuse women or children."

"When does he return?"

His lips curved just enough that she wanted to press a kiss to them. "I am not sure. A few weeks, perhaps."

They continued toward the keep and Merida looked up to the huge stone structure wondering how long it would be before she felt at ease. Never would she feel at home but, hopefully, one day she would not be filled with apprehension.

CHAPTER TWENTY-THREE

PAIGE WOKE TO her husband, Alec, dressing hurriedly. His face was like stone. He yanked a tunic on and then dug up a pair of breeches from a trunk. It was still dark outside and she wondered if he'd decided to join in a hunt.

"Why are ye up so early?" she asked, wiping the sleep from her face.

When he turned to her, a lock of hair fell across his eyes and he pushed it away. "A guard woke me with the news that Ethan is gone."

Her stomach tightened. If the man did something foolish, they could be plunged into another clan war. For whatever delusional reason, Ethan had a vendetta against Clan Ross and was intent on killing them.

"How long has he been gone?"

"The guard outside his door was knocked unconscious, so we are not sure. His replacement found him."

Alec neared the bed and peered down at her. Paige loved him, but had yet to find the courage to tell him so. What if something happened and she'd not said the words?

"Go back to sleep. I am sure we will either find him right away or not at all. Either way, ye will have news by the end of the day."

His lips met hers and as he kissed her, her eyelids fell. It was incredulous that she'd married the laird's son and slept in a plush bed with servants seeing to her needs.

Just a few months earlier, she'd lived with her brother and grandfather in a tiny cottage in the woods. The war had caused them to live on the brink of starvation, barely able to scratch out enough money for any kind of sustenance.

Although she continued to mourn for both of the most important men in her life, her husband filled a huge portion of the void. Her brother had been killed working as a messenger for the McLeods and her grandfather died quietly in his sleep soon thereafter.

She sat up. "Alec, why do ye have to go? There are plenty of guardsmen who can do it."

Instantly, his face turned hard. "Because I have had enough and if Ethan tries to kill any of my men, I shall slay him instead. He is not well. We should have known he'd do what he could to get free."

Alec went to a table where his sword and scabbard were and picked up the rustic items.

"Be with care," Paige said. "I…"

"I will be fine," Alec interrupted. "Until soon." He nodded and, an instant later, he was gone.

"Ugh," Paige mumbled, falling back onto the pillows. "I love ye," she murmured to the empty room.

Alec descended the stairs to find his father and several guards gathered. "Which direction did he go?" He hoped the answer would be anything but south, toward Ross lands.

"South," a guard replied. "Several scouts have gone after him already."

"Let us go." Alec looked at his father's haggard face. "I will do my best to bring him back alive, Da."

Even if they wished to, they could not track Ethan in the dark. Instead, they rode south hoping that once the sun rose, it would be easier. Although Ethan was a good warrior, he was not adept at keeping his tracks hidden and that gave Alec hope.

Whatever Ethan's objective was, surely it would not be a sensible one. His brother no longer thought logically. He was struck with some sort of madness that urged him to do irrational things.

A guard came alongside Alec. The warrior had once been very close to Ethan. However, one day at sword practice, Ethan had sliced the man across his left side. The action had brought on hatred between them. Alec knew the man was honorable and would not go against his father's wishes.

"Yer Da said that if it comes between ye and yer brother, I am to ensure ye survive."

There was a tightening in Alec's gut. "I hope it doesn't come to that."

"Neither do I." The guard's profile was grim. "Do ye know what happened to him?"

"Nay. I often wonder what caused my brother to become like he is. But then I recall the many odd things he did as a child. I think Ethan has always been a bit mad."

The man nodded. "Aye, in an angry way."

They rode in silence after that. The only sounds were the horse's hooves on the damp leaves and grasses.

Soon, the sun rose and Alec could only watch in wonder at the beautiful colors exploding on the horizon. Was Ethan somewhere nearby watching the sunrise? How could anyone not admire the gift of dawn?

Sadness filled him as he looked across the wide expanse of land before them. If they found Ethan, it would be a miracle. There was so much land to cover and not nearly enough men to do it.

Nonetheless, they spread out in ten groups of three men and continued forward.

⋙⋘

GISELA MUNRO EASED back against the wall. The man who'd entered her home in the middle of the night now sat on a chair. He was not well, his unfocused eyes roving continually around the room as if expecting someone to burst in at any moment.

Although hopeful the warrior she'd come upon just days earlier would be persistent and return, she doubted he would care enough to come see about her.

"Ye can leave now. The sun is up," Gisela whispered, trying her best to not sound scared.

The man was dressed well. He certainly was not a pauper by the quality of his clothing. However, he'd not been wearing a covering of any kind. In only a tunic and breeches, he seemed to have left wherever he came from in a hurry.

He did, however, have a sword, which he held.

"I will leave when I'm good and ready, wench," he snapped. She cringed when his gaze roved over her body. "Ye can lay in the bed. Perhaps I will join ye."

Although her legs ached from standing, she would rather die than allow him to touch her.

Just then, there was a soft creak as her overweight white cat, Milky, jumped from one of the chairs and made its way to the door. The animal preferred to spend the days outdoors, often sunning in front of the cottage. The cat meowed, demanding to be allowed out.

Gisela studied the small animal, wishing it would somehow realize she was in trouble.

Milky stared up at her and meowed louder.

"My cat wants to be allowed out," she said, hoping the man would do so and put down the sword.

"Does it now?" The man turned to the cat, which repeated its meowing request.

"Can ye please allow her out?" Gisela held her breath until the man stood and when he did not release the sword, panic set in as to what he might do.

The man stood and walked toward her. "I am not mad." His unfocused gaze said otherwise, but Gisela nodded as if agreeing with him.

"Please, let me go. Ye can remain here if ye wish." Her voice wobbled as she fought not to cry. The man was going to violate her, probably kill her as well.

"What is yer name?" the man asked, nearing. "Ye are a pretty sort, much too lovely to live alone."

"Gisela," she replied as she gauged what she could reach to strike him with, stretching her right hand slowly. When her fingers touched the edge of a bowl, she was deflated. What harm could she possibly do with a simple wooden item?

The man stopped just a hair's breadth away. "Ye are frightened of me." He seemed to find humor in it. "I can have any woman I wish for. My bed is never empty." His upper lip curled. "I want to eat."

Gisela scrambled sideways and grabbed the handle of a pot that held the cold remnants of her last meal. If he came close, she planned to swing it and hit him. Hopefully with enough force, he would be knocked unconscious.

"I have a bit of mutton stew left. If I start a fire..." She stopped speaking when he shoved her sideways and she fell, hitting her head on the table.

Panic gripped her as everything became blurry. Gisela screamed, or she thought she did, but then blackness took over.

ETHAN STOOD OVER the unconscious woman. "Cold mutton," he murmured and kicked at the pot that lay next to her on the ground. "There ye go cat, come and eat yer fill." He chuckled without mirth.

Not wanting to remain there any longer in case his father's warriors stumbled upon the cottage, he went outside and looked up at the sky. Storm clouds had formed and, soon, rain would begin falling.

Deciding he'd need to keep warm for a long as possible, Ethan went back inside and grabbed a thick blanket from the woman's bed. She still remained unmoving. Perhaps she was dead.

"Hmmm, too bad. Ye would have made a good bedmate." He rolled the blanket and then tied it to his horse's saddle. The animal had obviously had its fill of fresh grasses because it didn't take much coaxing to get it to a fast trot. He'd started off going south, but had since traveled northwest. Those that followed him would continue south thinking he headed to Ross lands.

He'd heard murmuring that Kieran Ross was at the northern post of Ross lands. If this were true, he would not be within the confines of the keep walls. It would be easier to bide his time and catch Kieran alone.

Once Kieran Ross was dead, Ethan would plan how to kill the other brothers. Perhaps, he'd kill the wife and daughter of the late Laird Ross as well. He shook his head. "No. I do not kill women." He considered that he may have just inadvertently killed one and chuckled. "That one does not count."

With a plan in mind, he urged his mount to a gallop, leaving the forest and the cottage behind.

"GISELA!" A WOMAN'S voice permeated and then she was being shaken. "What happened?"

Gisela opened her eyes and peered up at her mother. "I was pushed. A man came and he…" The room shifted as her mother pulled her up to sit.

"Oh, no. Did he…did he…" her mother stuttered, turning pale. "I knew it was a mistake for ye to live here alone."

"I could not remain living with ye and that man." The anger that surged, helped her come around and she scrambled to stand. Gingerly, she touched the back of her head where a bump had formed. "I am beginning to detest men."

Her mother was a plump woman with rosy cheeks who acted like a child. Although Gisela was sure her mother loved her, men always took precedence over her own children. After the last two had attempted to crawl into bed with Gisela, she'd run away and had lived with her grandmother in the cottage near the village. When her grandmother died, Gisela remained in the cottage.

She had one brother, Hamus, who worked for Laird Munro as a stable hand. Unfortunately, he couldn't take Gisela to live with him, nor did he have time to stop by regularly to ensure she was well.

That her mother came that day was surprising. The woman studied her. "Are ye feeling better?"

"Nay, my head hurts." Gisela lowered to a chair.

"Was it the warrior that ye quarreled with in the village the other day and scratched his face?"

A picture of the much too handsome and too arrogant man formed. "Nay. He would not lower himself to visit my cottage."

"Who was it then?"

"I do not know, Mother. He was young with clothing of good quality. I would say a rich man's son."

Her mother straightened. "Was he here to court ye then?"

Gisela gave her mother a flat look. "A man out to court does not shove a woman down and leave."

"True," her mother said, tapping her bottom lip. "Quite strange would ye not say?"

"Mother," Gisela snapped, holding back the desire to shake the woman. "He came to hide and may have had plans to do me harm if not for the fact I was prepared to fight back. It was not only strange, it was terrifying."

Her mother scowled. "Aye, of course. I came to tell ye it is safe to return home. Henry left. He just left. Forever," she added.

"It will not be long before another man moves in, I am sure," Gisela said, unmoved when her mother sniffed loudly. "I will not return only to have to leave again in a few weeks."

It was almost comical when her mother's despair quickly vanished. "Oh, the baker is a widower, ye know. He is most pleasant."

Picturing the rotund man, Gisela suppressed the shudder that threatened. "I require some items to make soap and would like to purchase herbs for a tincture." She stood slowly to ensure nothing shifted.

"To the village then?" her mother asked with a wide smile. "I will buy ye whatever is required. Henry never checked how much coin I took. I have plenty."

Her mother always had money. Her father had ensured they would not want for anything. As a merchant, he'd always made sure that they had enough coin and material possessions. Her mother had grown spoiled as he fulfilled her every whim.

Although Gisela had never wanted for anything, she'd not been as indulged, for which she was grateful now. Thanks to her father's good planning, her cottage was well-appointed with sturdy furniture that Hamus had acquired. The walls and roof were kept in good repair and in the small stable behind the structure, she had a horse and a cart that provided her with transportation to and from the village. She also had several chickens and two goats.

"How did ye get here?" Gisela asked, peering out the window. Although living only a few minutes' walk away, her mother would never do so.

"I walked," her mother announced proudly.

"All the way from yer house?"

"Oh, nay. Fergus Mackay was headed to visit his mother and kindly offered to bring me half of the way."

Gisela slid a look to her mother, but did not make another comment. “When we go to the village, I will inform Hamus about the man who came here,” she said, referring to her brother.

“Then we shall eat. Once ye purchase what ye need, of course.” Her mother became serious. “Ye will stay in the village until Hamus can come and ensure it is safe for ye to return.”

“Very well,” Gisela agreed.

Her mother motioned to her small bedroom. “Hurry, get dress. This is going to be an exciting day.”

CHAPTER TWENTY-FOUR

THE NEW HOME made Merida nervous. It was a large, half-empty house with many rooms and most of them without furnishings.

Tristan explained that, at one time, his uncle and wife had lived there. But upon his aunt's death, his uncle had burned most of the furnishings and moved into a chamber in the main house.

Apparently, in his grief, he'd attempted to erase every reminder of her, until stopped by the family.

The walls had been scrubbed and the main rooms on the lower level had rushes, wall hangings and all needed furniture.

That particular day, almost fourteen days since moving to *Dun Airgid*, she felt free to move about without worrying who would appear.

Merida and her maid wandered the upstairs as she planned what kind of furniture she'd have the carpenter construct. So far, there were three empty bedchambers, a sitting room and what looked to have been some sort of study.

Elsa sneezed. "I do not care for this place," the girl said, looking up at the rafters. "However, after everything is in place, I do suppose it will be lovely."

"Aye, I think so as well." Merida stepped over a rather ominous-looking pile. "Is that a wee corpse?" She peered down at it. "Some sort of beastie?"

Her companion squealed and jumped against the wall. "It is not dead."

A rather chubby cat uncurled and grumbled at being disturbed. It ambled away from them not the least bit fearful.

"Rather presumptuous," Merida said, watching it. "I do not believe this beastie is a mouser, but rather believes himself entitled."

Elsa peered at the creature. "A cat?"

"Yes, a cat." Merida moved closer to the animal, which meowed softly.

There were footsteps downstairs and Moira, the cook from the main house, called up. "I have come to help set up the kitchen. Tis taken me too long," she continued as Merida and Elsa hurried down the stairs. Merida looked over her shoulder at the cat that'd curled into a ball and had fallen fast asleep.

Moira and two maids carried baskets of pots, pans, spoons and other items. The red-faced, short woman ordered them about like a leader of the guard. Then she hesitated and looked around the room. "Where is Tom?"

"Who is Tom?" Merida asked.

"The mouser," Moira replied. "I brought him by to keep an eye on the kitchen."

"He is upstairs resting," Elsa said, pointing at the ceiling. "I do not believe he cares for working. Rather rotund is he not?"

"Aye, ye would be surprised how animated he becomes at spotting a mouse."

They continued helping with the set up of the kitchens. Moira introduced two girls who would be working there and Merida wondered if the fact the kitchen was being set up was to keep her away from joining at meals with the rest of Tristan's family.

"Moira, may I speak with ye?" Merida motioned for the woman to follow her out of the kitchen. Once in the corridor, she let out a breath. "Who ordered that the kitchen be set up? Are my husband and I to take all of our meals here then?"

The cook looked a bit uncomfortable. "Lady Ross. She said ye wished it."

Instead of contradicting the woman to a servant, Merida nodded and returned to the kitchen where the maids looked up with curiosity.

"We will break our fast and have midday meals here. However, do not plan to prepare last meal. My husband and I will go to the main house for it."

She stormed from the house to the larger one, not hesitating upon seeing Tristan and his brother along with their uncle in the great room. Instead, she went directly up the stairs to find her mother-in-law.

Both Lady Ross and Verity were in the sitting room. Upon her entrance, the women looked up, their eyes widening and then narrowing into slits.

"What do ye want?" Lady Ross asked with a sneer.

"My husband will not be excluded from this family. We will be taking last meal here every day, whether ye like it or not."

"I think it's time for us to get matters clear," Lady Ross said, smoothing her skirts. "This is my son's home. He can come and go as he pleases. Ye are the one who is not welcome here by anybody. Tis best if ye returned back to where ye came from."

A dagger sinking into her chest would have hurt less. What the woman said should not have hurt, but it did. Merida let out a ragged breath and lifted her chin.

"It was not my choice to marry yer son. I was forced into it, we both were."

"Then make a choice to leave," Lady Ross replied.

Verity, who'd remained silent, smiled at her as if she took glee in Merida's discomfort. "True. As Mother states, ye should just go."

"Sometimes, I wish I could," she replied, only to stop upon seeing that Tristan walked up. His eyes narrowed a bit at her. She wasn't sure how much he'd heard.

He walked into the room, immediately seeming to shrink the space. "Mother, do not meddle in my marriage or my house. Merida is my wife and ye will have to accept it."

"I do not." Lady Ross stood and somehow managed to look down at her son, her nose up in the air. "I tire of ye and yer brother bringing in women that are not worthy of this household. Tis not what yer father would have wanted for either of ye."

"My father is no longer here. Stop speaking for him. Ye know he would have done what was best for the clan."

The woman waved dismissively at Merida. "And that is best for this clan how?"

"Maintaining the peace. Not only that," Tristan turned to Merida. "I love this woman."

The floor shifted and Merida reached out to steady herself, her hand on Tristan's side. Had he said the words because he meant them or because he wished to shock his mother?

Lady Ross was struck silent, her round eyes moving from Tristan to Merida. "What did, what did ye say?" she stammered.

"That I love Merida," Tristan repeated. He slid a look to her, his eyes full of questions.

Merida's heart melted at his need for confirmation. "I love ye as well," she replied, not caring that the two women who hated her the most were witnesses to the first time they declared their love.

The corners of Tristan's lips twitched, as he must have been thinking the same. "Very well then. Mother, are we clear?"

"I am moving to the Munro keep upon Verity's marriage."

"I do not wish ye to feel unwelcome here, Mother, but ye have made it hard for both Elspeth and Merida to be comfortable. It is their home now as well."

The woman blew out a breath and looked up to the ceiling. "I will leave. I cannot abide remaining here. Perhaps I will take Kieran with me. He is the most sensible of all of ye."

Tristan scowled. "Kieran is barely civil. I doubt ye will convince him to do anything."

The woman pushed past them and down the corridor with surprising speed. "I will send a messenger and inform Kieran to return home immediately."

Verity, seeming at a loss, stood and gave Tristan a speculative look. "I hope ye will come to my wedding. I would like to have all my brothers there." Without looking at Merida, she brushed past.

"They planned to leave before ye came. Tis more of a show of disagreement that Mother brings it up again," Tristan explained.

Merida reached up to cup his face with both hands. "Did ye mean what ye said? Ye love me?"

His eyes met hers. "I do. I realized it when ye stabbed me through the heart with yer words a bit ago."

"What words?" Merida's breath hitched. "What did I say?"

"Wishing ye could go."

Leaning forward, she laid her head on his chest. "I do miss my home. My family. That is what I meant. I could never leave ye."

The steadiness of his heartbeat helped calm her. "Do ye think yer mother will come around?"

"In about one hundred years," he replied and lifted her face up to press his lips to hers. The tenderness he displayed with her was such a contradiction to who he was on the exterior.

Hard and emotionless, his façade rarely showing much more than a scowl, and yet with her, he was careful, gentle and took great care when touching her.

"Ye are such a good man," she said between kisses.

"I hope ye always think that." Tristan straightened. "I will arrange for ye to go visit yer family if ye wish. We have a truce, so traveling will not be as dangerous. Would ye like that?"

Merida grinned widely. "Yes."

He guided her down the stairs to the great room. "I am famished," Tristan said. "We did not break our fast this morning. Not with food anyway." He winked and heat filled her face, recalling how they'd made love until a guard had come to the house to fetch Tristan for a meeting of the council.

Chapter Twenty-Five

Rain pelted down upon the land and Merida grew weary of it. Saddened that the weather prevented her from traveling to visit her family, she scowled out the window.

It was late and despite the fire in the hearth, there was an uncomfortable chill in the air brought by the storm.

It didn't help that Elsa was in bed feeling poorly and the two maids they'd hired had gone to their chambers. Tristan was gone to nearby lands with his brother to bring several local farmers to an agreement.

Apparently, there was a quarrel between the men who'd had to resettle in their farms after the clan war ended. Borders and encroaching on others, along with cattle being stolen, made for many an argument.

Tired of pacing, she decided to go to the kitchens to find something to eat.

Tom, the cat, looked up from the corner of the room. But seeming to find her uninteresting, he went back to his napping.

At the back door opening, Merida assumed Tristan had returned. She whirled around to a large man filling the empty space.

A tartan that he'd pulled over himself in a useless attempt to stay dry hid his face. By the air of danger that seemed to emanate from him, she immediately guessed it wasn't Tristan but someone who may have come to kill her.

Frantic for a weapon, she reached for a wooden spoon and backed away, not stopping until her back slammed against a wall of shelves. A cup toppled from one and shattered on the floor.

The man was as tall as Tristan. There was little doubt it would be easy for him to overcome her.

Not seeming to notice her, he yanked the tartan off and threw it into a wet pile on the floor next to the cat's bed. Tom hissed, announcing his displeasure and the man peered down at the cat.

"What are ye doing here, woman?" He had a deep voice, not unpleasant. With hair down to his shoulders and, from what she could see, a short beard, he seemed rather savage.

Merida shrunk even further back, too frightened to formulate words.

"Who are ye? Why are ye here?" he repeated, still not looking at her.

"I am Merida, Tristan's wife."

The man jerked up to look at her and Merida lost her breath.

Before her was the most handsome human she'd ever seen in her life and, yet, at the same time, pure hatred emanated from him.

He had to be Kieran. She'd heard rumblings about him and how he looked from maids and also Elspeth, but they didn't sound true. Now, she knew everything said about his appearance was true. Actually, the tales of his beauty did him little justice.

"The McLeod's daughter." His upper lip curled in distaste as his eyes bored into hers.

Tears pricked and she did her best to keep them away. "Do ye mean to kill me?" Her voice trembled and she tightened her grip on the wooden spoon.

He let out a breath, but didn't reply. Instead, his heavily-lashed eyes locked on to the wooden spoon.

His gaze bored into hers. A deep hatred emanated from him and she lost her breath until he looked around the room as if measuring.

Kieran scowled. "I will not kill ye. Stay out of my way."

He turned and, after picking up the sopping wet tartan, went back out into the storm.

Merida slid down the wall until she was sitting on the floor, the spoon falling from her hand.

The thought of the lethal man hunting her brother sent a shiver down her spine. So much hatred saddened her and yet she understood that it must have been devastating for Kieran to witness his father being slain.

If the same had happened to her, she was sure revenge would be on her mind. But to what lengths would she carry it through?

Ethan was dangerous, in that he didn't touch his heart when going after an enemy. Her brother was without prejudice of whom he destroyed. As time passed, he became more distant of any emotion.

By what she had just witnessed, although obviously dangerous, Kieran Ross did possess a sense of right and wrong. It could be the weakness in him that Ethan would exploit.

Raindrops continued to fall in earnest and she prayed that Tristan was somewhere warm that night.

⋙⋘

A LAD WOKE upon Kieran entering the kitchens. He hurried to wake Moira who hustled in and began fussing over Kieran, as was her custom. She roused another lad and, soon after, a warm bath awaited him.

He didn't argue against it, as his entire body was soiled and cold.

Sinking into the tub, Kieran couldn't help but let out a long sigh. The heated water was like a balm and he allowed himself a few moments to allow it to seep into his body. Soon, it became almost impossible to remain awake.

When his head lolled to the side, Moira tapped him on the shoulder. "Come now, let's get ye dried and off to bed with ye."

The woman had always treated him as a lad and no matter that he was now almost thirty, she didn't change. There had been times when he'd snapped at Moira and hurt her feelings. Each time, he'd hurriedly apologized, not liking to hurt the kind woman who'd doted upon him since his birth.

Wrapped in a drying cloth, he trudged up the stairs, not looking forward to the day ahead. Time at home was time wasted. It was preferable to spend the days on the hunt for the man who'd killed his father.

Why did his brothers not seem to find it a priority?

Nonetheless, he had to be the one to hunt the bastard down. It was he who was to see the life leave Ethan McLeod's body. Part of the reason for returning home was to ensure everyone knew that.

Once in his bed, the familiarity of it pulled him to slumber. When the bed dipped, he knew one of the maids had been made aware of his return. Much too tired to care, he ignored her.

"I've come to see about yer needs," she murmured, her hand sliding down his stomach. Kieran's body stirred despite the exhaustion. It had been a long time since he'd been with a woman and when her hand wrapped around his staff, it didn't take long for him to become fully aroused.

The woman climbed atop him, straddled him and lowered, taking him in fully.

Kieran grasped her by the hips as she rode him at a steady pace. She moaned, leaning forward while pressing her palms on his chest and began to move faster.

He wasn't sure which one of the maids it was and didn't care. His body certainly didn't. Kieran closed his eyes as the woman's movements became frantic, the sound of flesh against flesh mingling with her moans.

A picture of a dark-haired woman formed. With bright pink lips and almond-shaped, brown eyes that flashed beautifully in anger, she had roused his interest.

"Oh," the maid cried out, her body shaking in release and she collapsed atop him.

With the picture in his mind of the woman he'd met in the north village, Kieran rolled the maid over onto her back, lifted her legs up over her head and plunged into her until fully seated. He continued to thrust until it was inevitable he was about to spill and pulled out, discarding his seed onto the bedding.

He released the now limp woman who tried reaching for his face. Pushing her hands away, he fell onto the bed face first. "Please go."

The maid ran her hand over his back. "I could stay and keep ye warm."

"No."

Moments later, soft footfalls were followed by the closing of his door. Kieran groaned as he settled into the pillow. Why had that particular woman returned to haunt him since meeting her?

She had not been a friendly one at that, but had actually scratched him across the face. True, he'd made a crude remark. But she had been friendly in a manner that he'd perceived as sexual interest. He tried to shrug off the incident, but time and time again, she'd come to mind. The beautiful soap seller who lived in a small village on Munro lands.

Wondering what her name was, he fell into an exhausted slumber.

CHAPTER TWENTY-SIX

TWO DAYS LATER, Tristan and Merida entered the great room. The room was filled. The clan's people who'd been unable to see Malcolm, for whatever matters they needed his attention for, had returned upon his.

Although Tristan assisted Malcolm most of the day, there was still much to do. Harvest time had to be considered. As houses were built for those displaced from the clan wars, people argued over who deserved to get one first.

His brother, who grew impatient with the constant quarreling, often stated, "Do as I say" and not giving any other explanations. In most cases, it was the only thing that could be said. It was impossible to make everyone happy.

Thankfully, at the moment, those in the room seemed to be calmed by the sight of food and the knowledge that they'd be sleeping in a warm place. He guided Merida to the front of the room, but she hesitated and looked to the back of the room.

A family sat huddled together at a table. The father was obviously ill, a constant coughing wracking his too thin body. The wife patted his back while trying to see after a crying babe in her arms and another two, who were still wee babes.

"Has anyone seen about them?" Merida asked, studying the family.

"Not yet. They wait to speak to Malcolm. Apparently, their cottage burned down and they've lost everything."

"I will see about them. If that is agreeable to ye?"

He sighed, knowing it was useless to say no. "As long as ye promise to come back and eat."

Merida nodded, already heading to where the family sat. Elspeth joined her and they began to speak to the family.

Already, they were housing too many people within the gates of the keep. Most were tradesmen and their families. Men that either produced goods or labor that benefited the clan were given a home and an area to work. It was obvious the sick man would not live much longer and the only thing he could offer was a widow and three orphans.

Farmers, herders and others lived in the surrounding lands or in the nearby villages would perhaps take the small family in.

Tristan settled next to Malcolm. "We should consider visiting the villages and seeing about settling people there. There is hardly any room left within the walls."

His brother studied Elspeth and Merida who were now each holding one of the young children and speaking to the parents. "We must put a stop to those two constantly finding ways to add people to live here."

Tristan nodded. "I agree."

Moments later, Elspeth had fetched the healer and, together, they escorted the sick man from the room.

Merida sat down with the woman, attempting to help feed the squirming children.

"Have ye considered when ye will have bairns?" Malcolm asked, looking at Tristan.

"Nay. Merida is not with child as yet. Have ye?"

"I believe Elspeth is already with child. However, she has not deemed to tell me. Perhaps she wishes to wait and be sure."

"Congratulations, Brother," Tristan said, meaning it. He studied Merida and wondered if she would tell him right away when she suspected or if she would be like Elspeth and wait.

In the morning, Kieran and he were to escort their mother and sister to Munro lands.

They meant to ensure their safe arrival and remain for the marriage ceremony. Since Verity and her mother had insisted on going to live with the Munros, it meant more carts and items to be taken.

A wedding ceremony would take place a day or so after they arrived. Tristan did not look forward to being away from Merida, but given the animosity between the women, it was not a good idea for her to go.

Just then, Naill entered and approached. "Laird, two of our guards went out to patrol to the west. Only one returned. He is barely alive."

"Where is he?"

"In the courtyard."

The brothers hurried out to the courtyard where the healer was already tearing the man's tunic away to inspect his injuries.

Just then, Kieran appeared, his face like stone as he looked down at the injured man. "Who did this?" he demanded of the pale man who groaned, obviously too far gone to form a coherent thought.

Tristan kneeled and took the man's hand. "Can ye speak?"

"Eth…Eth…an McLeod…McLeod…" The man's speech was slurred but he managed the words before his head fell sideways.

"He's dead," the healer said, his shoulders rounding. "Tis a wonder he lived long enough to come here."

"I will hunt that dog down." Kieran gritted out the words between clenched teeth. "I will find him and ensure he pays for every single thing he has done to our people."

"Ye will proceed to Munro lands as planned." Malcolm met both of their gazes and spoke in a low tone.

"Tristan, ye and twenty men will escort Mother and Verity." He turned to Kieran. "Ye and yer men will go ahead of them as planned. This is not the time to lose our heads. We do not wish harm to come to either our mother or our sister."

"Send others. Ye have plenty," Kieran said with a scowl.

Malcolm straightened, his angered expression concentrated on Kieran. "Ye will do as I say."

Like two bucks, the brothers sized each other up. They stepped away from the dead man, their gazes locked.

"Ye are wasting time hunting him alone. Ethan is mad. He will be his own undoing," Malcolm said between clenched teeth. "Ye are becoming as mad as he is."

Kieran swung, his fist barely missing Malcolm's jaw since the older brother expected it.

Taking advantage of the momentum, Malcolm sunk his fist into Kieran's midsection.

Kieran let out a loud oomph and doubled over. Within seconds, however, he swung again.

"Enough!" Tristan blocked Kieran's swing which hit him on the shoulder. His brother was quite strong so it sent Tristan back a couple steps. "Yer fighting will not solve the problem at hand. Malcolm is right. Ethan is mad. Given time, he will not be able to resist the opportunity to attack."

Kieran didn't seem convinced. "How many Ross' must die before we do something. Sending our men out has resulted in this." He motioned to the dead man who was now being carted away.

"So far, ye hunting him alone has not yielded any results either," Malcolm replied. "He is good at hiding."

"He is but one man," Tristan said. "Tis easy for him to remain unnoticed."

Kieran straightened. "He is heading to our northern border. Ethan must think that I am still at the post." His lips curved without mirth.

"This is a good thing."

Both Tristan and Malcolm knew it was useless to continue to argue with Kieran. He would do whatever he wished. Tristan's only hope was that Kieran didn't die because of his stubborn nature.

Then again, he, too, wanted revenge. Kieran had every right to avenge their father's death.

As everyone dispersed, he followed a still furious Kieran toward the stables. "Ye have every right to seek revenge, Brother. I, too, wish Ethan Ross dead."

"Then why do ye and Malcolm fight me every step of the way? Tis as if ye do not think I can accomplish it."

"If anyone can, it is ye. However, there are so many other matters at hand. We cannot allow Ethan Ross to be more important than the well-being of our people."

"Tell that to the dead man's family." Kieran stalked away.

"SO SOON?" THE food on Merida's plate lost its appeal and she fought not to cry. Her plans to see her mother hadn't worked out and now that Tristan had to go away again, she would have to wait longer before going home.

It wasn't Tristan's fault, but she was angry just the same. Everything was about his family. They came first and although she knew it was unreasonable to resent it, she did. For almost an entire season, she'd not seen her mother or father. She missed Paige and even her father's hounds.

"I promise to take ye to visit yer family upon my return." Tristan covered her hand with his. "Do not be sad."

Noting she was not eating, he leaned away from the table. "Perhaps we should go to our house. I must prepare since we depart early."

Lady Ross spoke animatedly to Verity and Elspeth. "Yer mother seems in good spirits."

"Aye. She looks forward to moving, I suppose. She and Lady Munro are good friends. I fear the Munro will build a bigger home as people are spilling out of the current home."

"And now yer mother and sister are going to live there as well," Merida said, wondering what the appeal was.

"Mother is taken by Lady Munro's affinity for entertaining. One of the reasons there are so many people there is the constant celebrations."

"Yer mother likes festivities then?"

"And the gossip they bring," Tristan replied.

She studied the woman who seemed relaxed despite the fact that she was about to leave her home. Eating with gusto and signaling for more mead, she chatted with her daughter, not seeming to run out of things to say.

"How do ye feel about her leaving?" Merida studied her husband who gave a one-shouldered shrug.

"Everything changed after Da was killed. This is a natural progression, I suppose. Malcolm, Kieran and I will form the new Clan Ross. Our families will grow here and we will set new traditions."

Not only had Ethan's actions changed the Ross Clan forever, but also the McLeod Clan. People had died and now new traditions and families formed. Although change was inevitable, the fact that it was precipitated by an irrational act made it seem all so unfair.

"Can we go home now?" she asked, leaning against Tristan. Suddenly, she was exhausted and wished for nothing more than to snuggle against the man she loved. Tomorrow, he would leave for days on end.

There was a bit of comfort that at least she would have Elspeth, Ceilidh and Elsa for company.

Upon entering their chamber, Tristan took her by the shoulders and met her gaze. "I do love ye, Merida, and will always return to ye."

"See that ye do," Merida replied. Without breaking eye contact, she unlaced her bodice and pushed her top down her shoulders.

Tristan watched with hooded eyes. His breathing hitching at her breasts coming free of the constraints and visible through the thin fabric of the chemise. Emboldened by the parting of his lips, she removed her top and then untied her skirts, letting the folds of fabric fall and pool at her feet.

The thin strap of her chemise fell off her right shoulder, the flimsy item barely concealing her nudity.

"Come to me," Merida said, walking backward to the bed. "I want ye, Husband."

Tristan yanked the belt from his waist, his breeches falling to his ankles. He fell upon her, his hard sex protruding and hard against hers.

With one hard thrust, he entered her and both of them cried out at the wonderful feeling.

CHAPTER TWENTY-SEVEN

DAWN ARRIVED AS Kieran rode, breaking through the trees to an open meadow. He'd slipped out quietly, not wanting to rouse the household and have another argument with Malcolm.

Just thinking about the day before filled him with rage. How could his brothers be so passive about Ethan Ross remaining alive?

The man would die and, if he guessed correctly, it would be soon.

In the distance, the outline of the small village meant he neared Munro lands. The Ross' and the Munros had always been friendly to one another and now that his sister was about to marry one of the laird's sons, it meant a bond was made.

In Kieran's opinion, it was a good thing since it meant strong allies now formed almost a complete circle around McLeod lands.

If any kind of war began, the McLeod would be at a severe disadvantage. Strange that the women of his family seemed to be the ones doing something that was helpful against the McLeod.

He slowed the pace of his horse as they ambled at the edge of a wooded area. The closer he got to the northwest border, the more careful he had to be. Kieran studied the surroundings for any signs of human travel.

Some broken twigs on the ground meant someone had come by

there not very long before him. Kieran dismounted to get a closer look.

AFTER SPENDING THE night at a village on Munro lands, Kieran rose and went to fetch his horse, Laith, from the stables. There was already activity in the center of town, people preparing for the day.

As he led his mount away from the center of town, he watched for any signs of the dark-haired woman, but she was nowhere to be seen.

No matter, it was for the best that any notions of a woman not distract him. Especially now, since there was too much at stake.

In the distance, he spotted a woman. Pulling her skirts up, she ran as if the devil himself chased her.

Kieran narrowed his gaze and scanned the surroundings. No one was pursuing her. She didn't look back but, instead, continued forward in the direction of the Munro keep.

Finding the sight interesting, he watched her as she seemed not to be in any danger, but more as if she had urgency to get wherever she went.

Her hair fell from its bindings, the dark curls blowing back away from her face. She glanced over her shoulder, not seeing him.

It was the soap maker.

The woman he'd been thinking about. And she was in a desperate hurry to get somewhere.

The End

About the Author

Most days USA Today Bestseller Hildie McQueen can be found in her overly tight leggings and green hoodie, holding a cup of British black tea while stalking her hunky lawn guy. Author of Medieval Highlander and American Historical romance, she writes something every reader can enjoy.

Hildie's favorite past-times are reader conventions, traveling, shopping and reading.

She resides in beautiful small town Georgia with her super-hero husband Kurt and three little doggies.

Visit her website at www.hildiemcqueen.com
Facebook: HildieMcQueen
Twitter: @HildieMcQueen
Instagram: hildiemcqueenwriter

Made in the USA
Columbia, SC
17 January 2020